"You need to climb up. Can you do that?"

"Y-yes. I think. It's hard to tell with the darkness."

Tru felt the wall with one hand, seeking something that would give him leverage. "I'm going to try to take my weight off the rope. I'll hold as long as I can while you climb."

"But what about you? I won't know how to fix this."

"I've seen you climb. I know you can do this." Maybe letting go of the rope and jumping would be better.

The grinding sound returned, canceling his thoughts. His rope dropped at least half a foot and caught again. It rested, but before he could take another breath, a large crack echoed through the chamber and he hurtled to the floor below.

"Out of the way!" He landed hard on his back but knew what was coming next.

At 185 feet above, a large boulder with an anchor and rope attached was about to come crashing down. Where it landed was anyone's guess.

Katy Lee writes suspenseful romances that thrill and inspire. She believes every story should stir and satisfy the reader—from the edge of their seat. A native New Englander, Katy loves to knit warm woolly things. She enjoys traveling the side roads and exploring the locals' hideaways. A homeschooling mom of three competitive swimmers, Katy often writes from the stands while cheering them on. Visit Katy at katyleebooks.com.

Books by Katy Lee

Love Inspired Suspense

Warning Signs
Grave Danger
Sunken Treasure
Permanent Vacancy
Amish Country Undercover
Amish Sanctuary
Holiday Suspect Pursuit
Cavern Cover-Up

Roads to Danger

Silent Night Pursuit
Blindsided
High Speed Holiday

CAVERN COVER-UP

KATY LEE

LOVE INSPIRED SUSPENSE

INSPIRATIONAL ROMANCE

LOVE INSPIRED® SUSPENSE

INSPIRATIONAL ROMANCE

Recycling programs for this product may not exist in your area.

ISBN-13: 978-1-335-58716-9

Cavern Cover-Up

Love Inspired
22 Adelaide St. West, 41st Floor
Toronto, Ontario M5H 4E3, Canada
www.LoveInspired.com

Printed in U.S.A.

Therefore whosoever heareth these sayings of mine,
and doeth them, I will liken him unto a wise man,
which built his house upon a rock.
—*Matthew* 7:24

To Staci, my go-to person
for everything Carlsbad Caverns National Park.
Thank you for your help!

ONE

Danika Lewis clicked on the hidden camera in her night goggles to record her eureka moment. After eight years of learning the ropes of private investigating, she believed she had just found her father's stolen treasure—or at least part of it. There was one item she was looking for that was not here.

Scanning the secret lode of Native American artifacts that her late father had spent his entire archaeological career unearthing, Danika never thought she would find it locked in a vault beneath a three-story San Antonio mansion while an engagement party roared above. Apparently, all those dry investigating classes paid off—and so had the photography lessons. She clicked the first shot just as a creaking sound captured her attention.

Danika glanced toward the open steel door that resembled a smaller version of that of a bank's and listened to hear if someone had tracked her down into the basement. She was supposed to be photographing the event as her undercover guise. She worked hard to get the recommendation from the wedding planner, and to come so far only to be caught in the moment of her find would be crushing. Not to mention it took her weeks to figure out the code. After all the possible codes Danika thought the vault's lock might be, she couldn't believe Dr. Martin Elliot locked up this priceless collection with his daughter's birth date. It almost felt too easy…like she was supposed to find it…and be caught.

A sinking feeling had Danika's mind whirling with a plan B.

She slunk toward the door, and with her back against the wall, she turned her ear to listen for any other sound coming from the basement theater. Outside the door stood ten rows of theater seats for the Elliots' private viewing room. Danika couldn't grasp the level of wealth this family had. It made her wonder if her father's findings contributed to Dr. Elliot's bottom line. And if that were the case, would she even find what she was looking for?

What if he'd already sold it on the black market?

As an elongated silence ensued outside the vault, she decided to resume her search. But this time, she picked up her pace. Something didn't feel right. But then, that feeling could be from the fact she was breaking and entering while she was supposed to be taking pictures of the party above. Being a PI didn't always pay the bills. That's where her photography skills came in handy, especially when she was investigating the people on the other side of the camera. Landing the Elliot wedding would lead her to her father's killer. Danika was sure about it.

And she wouldn't let a little creaking sound that

was probably someone dancing around upstairs stop her now.

Stepping up to a glass case filled with 600 AD turquoise gems and arrowheads from the tenth century, she shook her head in disgust. These artifacts had no business being locked away in a basement. The purpose of Danika's father's excavation was never to sell on the black market or to keep for himself what belonged to the native nations. And what was before her wasn't even the half of it. She estimated his collection should be about forty thousand pieces. She scanned the room for one object in particular. It was the object her father spent the greater part of his archaeological career seeking. It was also the object he was murdered for right after he found it. If she had done her investigation correctly, then the undated Pueblo eagle-feather masked headdress, with its long black-and-white feathers and a wooden beak for the mask, would be here.

Danika moved her head slowly around the room so the camera would catch each artifact clearly. She thought of how her father, Dr. Jared Lewis, had trusted his colleague Martin Elliot with his life. Since her dad's death, she often wondered if his own friend had killed him. She went into private investigating to learn the truth. And seek justice.

If he was involved, Danika would do whatever it took to make sure the great archaeologist was stripped of his credentials and never received the prestige and honor that should have gone to her father. Dr. Elliot would be forever ruined, while doing hard time. She would make sure of it.

She moved left to right and top to bottom, perusing

the glass encasements and shelves. She made it around the ten-by-ten room and came up empty-handed.

No masked headdress.

With no time to get frustrated, Danika turned back and scanned the walls. Any crack or impression that could be evidence of another secret room was also nowhere to be seen. Her camera's SD card had about an hour of footage available, but she had less time than that. The people upstairs would notice her disappearance soon, if they hadn't already. As the future couple's wedding photographer, Danika couldn't disappear for long. Sabrina Elliot would take notice. The bride's expectations exceeded reality. To secure the job as the photographer, Danika had to promise a photo collection worthy of a princess. Thankfully, the wedding planner vouched for her, as Danika had made a name for herself in the wedding circuit. But it also made for a great undercover disguise. No one would question her photographing the guests or house. What better way to snoop than from behind the camera? Also, being the photographer, nobody thought it strange to have her hanging around them and hearing their conversations. She was virtually invisible.

But she couldn't be too invisible, or the bride would come looking for her.

Danika closed her eyes to push away the idea that eight years of her research could be dashed away by a whiny debutant. Danika couldn't blow her cover now. She knew Brina and her oil tycoon fiancé, Terrence Lindsay, the son of Dr. Elliot's financier, had the means to not only ruin the investigation but also her life.

Taking this investigation on came with an understanding that she was risking everything, even her own trust fund her father left her—the last of his financial worth. When he died, he had nothing left, and Danika knew his killer ruined him in every way. She could have no missteps, or the same would happen to her. She also knew nothing was as it seemed.

The reminder had her moving stealthily around the room again, this time feeling the walls with her gloved hands. Along with the night goggles, she wore a wig of short blond hair that hid her dark brown waves; a black cap on top of that. Her typical photography outfit was all black, so no need to change while she snooped. Her uniform allowed her to be inconspicuous in a crowd of elaborately dressed guests, while also giving her the ability to disappear into the shadows…or down the stairs to the basement, as needed.

She swept her hand along the wall until she came to a shadow box with a turquoise necklace on display. She lifted the box from its place and froze at the sight of a small cubby cut into the wall. A large brown book had been placed inside. Putting the shadow box down on the floor, she withdrew the book and realized it was an old photo album.

Why hide a photo album in the wall?

Unless the memories were to be kept a secret.

Looking behind her at the open door, she listened intently to be sure she was still alone. She'd come for the headdress and wondered if she was crossing the line into something that was none of her business.

But what if there was a clue to connect Dr. Elliot

to her father's death? This might be her one chance to find out.

Danika took the album out and opened it wide on the glass display case in the middle of the room. Page after page were photos of excavations, most seemed legit with appropriate markings at the sites. Her father had his own collection of photographs. It was part of the digging business.

So why hide the album away?

She turned the pages and came to a few with people. Some were very old. She paused at a photo of an old 1950s picture of a sorority group. The eight ladies were dressed in white gowns and lined up with bouquets in their hands. They were in a cave with beautiful stalagmites and stalactites surrounding them. Danika instantly recognized the cavern room as the King's Palace in Carlsbad Caverns. She hadn't been to New Mexico in a few years. Not since she lost her rock-climbing partner to a fall in one of the caves. After that, she hadn't wanted to go there, but she would need to in three weeks. Brina was set to have her wedding there in the amphitheater.

The bride had whined about not being able to have the wedding in the King's Palace, as the park only allowed weddings outside in the amphitheater. Seeing this picture led Danika to wonder if there was more to Brina's choice. Who were these ladies in the picture? Family? But why hide them away in a vault?

Danika would investigate that later. For now, she moved on to the next page, only to pause again and inhale sharply. In this photo, her father stared at the camera with a group of six other men and one woman.

Were they all archaeologists? Danika wondered, but the face of Dr. Elliot stole her attention.

She knew she shouldn't be surprised Martin had a photo with her dad, but she wondered if this photo was why the man kept the album hidden. Was she staring at her father's killer? She had to believe one or more of these people were responsible for his death.

But how?

Did they all get a portion of the lode?

A noise on the stairs pulled her attention. But instead of closing the book and putting it back, she raced through the rest of the album, recording the pictures to study later. There were maps and people, as well as a catalog of special finds.

Placing the album and box back on the wall, she listened intently for any other sounds. Flattening against the wall by the door, she angled her head to see outside the room. She would need to pass through the personal theater's ten rows of comfy recliners and out to the rear patio. But if someone was waiting outside the door, she wouldn't make it halfway across the room.

There were no lights on, but Danika had memorized every piece of furniture and obstacle when she had entered the room, just as she would any rock wall she was about to climb. Every rock was a problem waiting to be solved, and once she did, she could do it blindfolded. She knew she could walk through this room blindfolded in record time if she had to. She bent to her knees and exited the vault. Pressing close to the wall, she noticed her goggles didn't pick up any movement. She expected the lights to be turned on any second and took the moment to spider-crawl across to the first row of recliners. She reached the end and stopped, checking carefully that no one thwarted her plan of escape and was waiting for her on the other side.

The coast was clear, straight through to the rear exit that would lead to the patio, the same way she entered.

"I've released the dogs," a man spoke from the staircase. His voice held an air of superiority, but it didn't sound like Dr. Elliot. One of his guards, maybe? Whoever it was, he thought he had her cornered.

Danika imagined the two Doberman pinschers waiting for her outside and unzipped the pouch at her waist. Slowly and without a sound, she reached in and felt for the snacks she'd brought just in case this happened. She'd met Brina's dogs and learned their favorite treat was bacon. She only hoped she could make it past them before they finished eating.

"You might as well reveal yourself. You can't stay down here forever, and there's no other escape now. Come out, and maybe I'll go easy on you. Maybe."

The lights flicked on, illuminating the basement.

Danika crouched lower behind the first large chair. She knew the cops would not be called, not when Dr. Elliot had a vault full of stolen artifacts. She had no intention of finding out what this henchman would do to her. Filling her lungs and closing her eyes, she envisioned the route she would take through the theater, around the far side of the chairs, and to the back exit. She would do it crouched low. Years of rock climbing at some of her father's digs and then in college on the rock-climbing team made her nimble and quick.

It would help her with the dogs too.

A stair tread creaked.

So the man was still on them…and coming down now. Danika stayed put, waiting to know the direction the man would take through the theater. Then she would crawl up the opposite side and out the door. Except, as she heard the man walk slowly down the stairs, he didn't come down the other side of the room. He was coming down the same side she was on.

Danika dropped her head back against the recliner, thinking of how she could deter him from coming this way. She reached into her pack on her waist and took out a small flashlight. Getting ready to run, she tossed it across the room in the direction she wanted the man to go. It smacked against a side table, and when she heard him race to that side, she took off up the side of the chairs toward the double doors. But before she burst through them, she heard the man speak. But not to her.

"She's heading your way," he said to someone else. Someone who she apparently was about to meet. He'd radioed ahead. "Blond hair, black hat and clothes."

He also knew she was a female. But did he know her true identity? Had she blown her cover? She thought she had taken care of all the cameras but must have missed one. How else could he have known she was down here?

Danika couldn't worry about that right now. She had to keep moving forward with her carefully laid-out plan and hope she didn't miss any other pertinent details. Brina would also be looking for her soon. The party was going on upstairs, and Brina probably wanted to memorialize another toast. The last two weren't enough. The woman liked to hear herself talk.

Danika focused on getting outside and back to her preparation room on the third floor. She had requested a private space for all her equipment—and getting in and out of her disguise.

The exterior door loomed ahead. The dogs were barking so loud, she could practically hear them salivating.

Danika reached into her pack and grabbed the whole lot of bacon. She opened the door wide enough to hold it at their noses. The barking stopped, and she pushed the door wide and threw the bacon to her left. They followed the meat, and she went right.

The palatial manor was three stories high and shaped like the letter *H*. Her guest room was on the top floor at the front of the house, but she couldn't head that way right away. Not until she knew no one was following her. They were probably figuring out right about now that the dogs didn't attack as they were supposed to. That gave her two minutes...maybe.

Danika kept herself shielded in the shrubs, glancing back after each one she moved to to be sure she was still alone. At the foot of the house, her room remained dark above, and she saw her window was still cracked open. The curtains billowed in the soft evening breeze. Feeling the wall for the first handhold, she took one last look behind her to see no one was there and lifted her body up. She'd memorized every foothold and hand placement, and in less than one minute scuttled up the side of the stucco house and into her bedroom window. As she passed through, she heard Brina's impatient voice behind the bedroom door.

"Danika, are you sleeping? This is highly unprofessional. Open up this instant!"

Danika shut the window and locked it. She tore the wig and goggles from her head and pulled the elastic to let her hair go free down her back. She removed her gloves and black leather coat, stashing them in the vanity's drawer. "Hold on, Brina," she said. "Just changing lenses."

Danika put her suit coat back on and slipped the three buttons back into place. One look in the mirror on the vanity and she smoothed out her hair and rushed toward the door, grabbing the camera from the bed. She secured it around her neck, ready to snap a photo as she swung the door wide.

Click.

Brina held her hand up. "I don't think you're funny." The bride-to-be didn't look amused, tilting her perfectly coiffed blond head, then crossing her bare arms, flashing a thick tennis bracelet at her wrist.

Danika held the camera out to show her the picture. "But you take the best photos, even when you're angry."

Brina pushed the camera away and pursed her lips. "You are fired. Do you understand me? And you will never work a wedding again. My father will make sure of it. You missed his toast downstairs."

Two concerns arose in Danika. One, she needed to be at that wedding, and two, would Dr. Elliot suspect that she was the one in the basement?

"Brina, you really don't want to fire me." Danika tried to think fast. What could she say to make the bride keep her on?

"Oh, yes I do. There are plenty of photographers who would gladly take your place."

"But none of them can get you into the King's Palace for the ceremony," Danika said on a rush, then cringed inwardly at her false claim.

Well, not totally false. There was a way. It was slim, and she would hate doing it, but to find her father's killer, she would do what she had to…even contacting the man she held responsible for her friend's death.

Brina paused, looking to be considering Danika's offer. "How?"

"I know someone who works at the park."

Brina squinted her fake lashes as she raised her slender, pointed chin. "Why haven't you mentioned this before? The wedding is in three weeks. You knew I preferred the King's Palace over the amphitheater."

"I didn't want to get your hopes up until I knew for sure. It was going to be a surprise tonight. And now you've ruined it. But, of course, this is only if I'm your photographer." Danika held her breath as she waited to hear if she would be shown the door or allowed to stay on and continue her investigation.

Brina held out her hand to take the camera. "Let me see my picture."

Danika turned the camera around to show her the quick shot she had taken moments ago.

Brina smiled at her image. "That *is* nice." She sighed and turned. "Fine. You can stay. But get downstairs. The fireworks are about to start, and I want those images to be part of the collection you promised."

Danika let out her own sigh, this one of relief. She

followed the bride-to-be, back in her undercover role as photographer and ready to survey the room of guests.

Brina giggled on the stairs then called out, "Daddy! You'll never guess what Danika has given me for my gift tonight. I'm getting married in the King's Palace!" She raised her arms high in delight and squealed.

As people below cheered in awe, Danika thought about the mountain she would have to climb to make this happen. This wall was insurmountable. She had a big problem to solve when it came to Truman Butler. She couldn't even be sure if he would remember her. And if he did, he would remember he didn't like her at all.

But that was okay because she didn't care for him either.

Truman Butler rappelled up the narrow hundred-foot dirt hole in the dark Lechuguilla Cave in Carlsbad Caverns, New Mexico. His watch told him it was late morning, but he hadn't seen daylight in four days.

"Off rope!" he shouted down for his fellow park ranger Kip Sylvester to begin his ascent next.

"On rope!" Kip hollered up from below, and the ropes went taut with the man's weight.

Tru crouched low in the small chamber as he waited for his partner before progressing toward the opening of the cave. He turned off his headlamp on his brimless yellow hard hat, and his surroundings went completely black. Battery power must be saved at all costs in the caves. There was nothing worse than a dimming headlamp inside these precarious tunnels.

One wrong dark step could be his last—a lesson he learned the hard way.

Tru pushed down the memory that would plague him until his dying breath. Instead, he used the lesson to fuel his mission here at Carlsbad Caverns National Park. Rules were in place for safety, and he made sure they were abided by at all times.

Off in the distance, he could make out a shimmer of light. They were almost back to the mouth of Lechuguilla. Long before the surveying began into the cave, the entry was called Old Misery Pit. It used to be nothing more than one of the many deep holes of melted limestone that dotted the desert floor. But the amount of air blowing from the hole had warranted an exploration. Teams were created to probe and map out the extent of the cave. That was fifty years ago, and they had yet to make a dent into the enormity of its size. It's been said the find would be like discovering Yellowstone in your backyard. The break into this cavern was one of the most important discoveries ever made by the caving community. When the survey was finally complete, records for length and depth would be broken. Tru knew as long as there were speleologists and cavers willing to press themselves into tight chambers and rappel into deep holes, the other end would be found eventually. He also knew lives would be lost in the process. That fact never made it any easier when he had to organize a recovery instead of an exploration. Especially when that recovery was the woman he was supposed to marry.

Kip popped his head up out of the hole, and the blinding light from his headlamp put his face into shadow. "I'm getting tired," he said and huffed out a weary breath. "My arms are shaking."

"Then we rest." Tru sat down right where he was to wait it out. "There are no heroes in caves." He opened his side pack of supplies and removed his water canteen. His rationed amount left just a few more swigs. He took only one. He would always save his last gulp for when he exited the cave. Anything could happen before then.

"I don't know how you cavers do this. Going down into the belly of the earth for no reason." Kip laughed and took a long drink from his own canteen.

"*You* cavers?" Tru felt his blood boil. "I was under the impression you had experience. Why exactly did you sign up?" This whole expedition was a waste of money and resources. It was no wonder he had barely made any headway into the cave.

"I do have experience, just nothing to this gargantuan size. I've done some rescues, but typically stay close to the opening. I think I need to keep to that. You know? That might be where my heart lies."

Tru let a bit of his anger go. He may have lost time and money, but at least he didn't lose any lives. The trek was successful in that regard. "I suppose we all have our reasons for this lifestyle. Mine is to map out the workings of the tunnels. It's not for me, but rather future people who come through here."

"A guide sure does help to keep people alive." Kip put his canteen back in his pack. "I think I'm ready."

Tru turned on his light to see Kip's face. The man was sweating profusely, which wasn't necessarily uncommon for him. The New Mexico heat always bothered him, and he carried around a cloth to swipe at his brow numerous times a day. But the caves were a constant cool fifty-six degrees year-round. "You have to be sure. Not just think so." Tru's direction left no room for negotiation. "Honesty only."

At Kip's nod, the two of them set out in a spider-like crawl toward the light. As the chamber opened up, they stood to their full height. Tru noticed Kip lagging a bit and slowed his step. Allowing Kip to go on ahead of him, Tru watched his cave buddy tripping over the rock crevices.

"You're getting sloppy," Tru said.

"I'm fine. We're almost there." Kip kept moving.

"Most accidents happen near the end. I think you need to slow down."

"I just want to get out of here. Maybe I'm not cut out to be a ranger at Carlsbad. You don't mind it down here, but this darkness gives me the creeps. I'll take the mountains any day."

"I hear you. I grew up in Taos. I mapped Mount Wheeler with my brother." He cleared his throat at the thought of his older brother, Jett. He missed those days. "It's the mapping that I love. It's knowing that people who follow behind me will always have a guide to lead them. You have to know why you've chosen this profession. It becomes your mission."

"Yeah, well, I think I'll stick to patrol aboveground. Or give me a safe desk job." Kip laughed nervously and stumbled.

"We need to stop," Tru said.

But the next second Kip fell to his side.

Tru shot out a hand and caught him before he fell

into a black void. "We slow down. Before you fall down." Kip was weak, but Tru held him up the rest of the way. By the time they broke through into sunlight, Tru was past irritated. Kip had not been ready for such a treacherous cave, if any cave at all. Going from the coolness of the caverns into ninety degree spring desert heat didn't help Tru.

He left Kip to the medical personnel, there to assist cavers coming out of their expeditions. Many cavers emerged with dehydration and injuries. It came with the territory. Tru made his way to his tent that was set up on the site. It wasn't his main office at headquarters, but he spent more time in the cave than he did in the building.

As he stormed toward the flaps, he could see his assistant waving him down by one of the park pickup trucks. Needing a moment to breathe, he avoided her and went inside the tent. Whatever she had to tell him could wait until he knew that he wouldn't take his anger out on her. Why had he thought Kip could make the trek? They barely added any distance to his map. Another expedition would have to be made. He opened his canteen and drained the last of the water... and froze.

Over the green container, he noticed he wasn't alone.

A stranger was in his tent.

Tru lowered the bottle slowly. A woman with long brown hair and dressed in athletic wear stood over his cartography table. His latest map of the cave spread wide. He often wondered how many tables he would need by the time this cave was fully explored.

He couldn't see the woman's face as her hair hung in waves in front of it.

"I hope you have a good reason for sneaking in here," Tru said, tempering his anger as best he could.

The woman lifted her face to him. She had a look of determination that he recognized. She was also quite stunning with her piercing blue eyes that cried out to be explored deeper.

"My name is Danika Lewis." She stopped there, as if any further explanation for her presence in his private space was unnecessary.

"Okay. And?" The edge in his voice expressed his irritation at this intrusion. "Is that supposed to mean something to me?"

Her eyebrows rose over those interesting eyes, and she huffed. "No. I guess not." She mumbled something about not being surprised.

"Excuse me?" Tru leaned an ear her way. "I missed what you said."

"Never mind that." She shook her head, sending her hair in a swaying wave. It reminded him of a certain rock on the park's land that years of wind had carved out into the perfect curve. Her hair looked just as smooth. "I'm a professional photographer, and I've been told you're the man I must speak to," she continued and pulled his attention back to her reason for being here.

"About what?" Tru moved farther into the tent and came around the other side of the table. His working map sprawled open between them as they faced off with more than this cave of uncertainty between them. This woman had snuck into his space. For someone who was used to cramped places, he wondered why he struggled to breathe with her in his proximity. "How could I possibly be of help to you?"

"I have a couple requests, but first, I want to hire you as a guide into some caves."

"There are plenty of guides you can hire. As head ranger of surveying, I don't do that. I inspect and survey uncharted caves." He referenced the map between them.

"The caves I need to go into are restricted. I need you to break the rules and take me through them."

"I never break the rules."

She scoffed under her breath. "That's not what I heard."

Tru paused at her words. His throat went dry. How did she know? No one knew. The only person who knew what he did was gone forever. Dead because he broke the rules. This woman had to be bluffing.

"You're mistaken." His voice sounded hoarse.

She frowned and looked to a place past him and toward the tent's closed flaps. Her saddened expression mirrored his pain, but how could that be possible? This Danika Whoever-She-Was didn't know his Melinda. He found himself growing angry at her intrusion, not only into his tent but also into his heart.

"If you'll excuse me, I really need to get back to work. You'll have to find another guide." Tru moved to his desk, averting this unnerving woman's piercing eyes and giving her his back.

"I said I have a couple requests," she spoke from the same place. "One is a guide, and the other a request to move a wedding that will be taking place here in three weeks from the amphitheater to the King's Palace. I'll be photographing the event of a well-known archaeologist's daughter."

Tru sputtered and whipped around to face her again. "That is a definite no. There are no weddings allowed in the caves. I don't care who they are. No compromise."

"I'll pay extra. I'll make a large donation to the..." She looked down at the opened map on the table. "Exhibition you're working on." She lifted her gaze back to him. "How much will it take to get you where you want to be?"

Tru thought about the hoops he would have to go through to set up the exploration he really wanted to lead. All these little treks barely got him a few feet farther inside the cave. As his mind whirled with numbers, his common sense took over.

Thankfully.

"Well?" she asked.

Tru shook his head. "I can't help you. Not with a wedding or as your guide. I'm not breaking the rules and taking you into restricted caves. I work all day long keeping people out of them. So, if that's all the requests you have, you can go. I've been in a cave for days, and I need to get cleaned up and get some real food in me." He turned and headed toward his wooden chest in the corner.

The woman followed on his heels. "Okay, fine, but if I show you some photos, can you tell me which cave they are from? I'll go by myself."

He grabbed a clean shirt and turned back. "Lady, people have died in these caves. This is not an amusement park. It's nature, and nature can be cruel." Glancing down, he noticed he had the cotton T fisted tightly in his hand.

She noticed his fisted hand too. She took three tentative steps back. "It's Danika, Danika Lewis, not that the name means anything to you. I'm sorry to bother you."

"Wait. I didn't mean to snap. It's just I've seen what these caves can do. It's no joke."

She put up her hands to stop him. "I understand. I didn't think it would hurt to ask. Apparently, I was wrong." She left before he could say another word, not that there were any words to change his thoughts… or his fears.

Then he thought of her words, *I'll go by myself*, and he noticed his hand trembling. The distance to the tent flaps where she had just exited seemed so far away. "You don't understand the dangers," he said aloud.

Danika Whoever-She-Said-She-Was could be walking toward her death.

TWO

Danika made her way back toward her SUV parked along the winding road that led to the cave. Truman Butler was just as handsome as she remembered with his short haircut that grew a bit longer on top. His black hair and tan skin reflected some Native American heritage in his genes. But the eyes she remembered were different.

His green eyes that used to look at her friend with adoration were now cold as ice.

As Danika worked to forget the man again, she unlocked the door and noticed the woman ranger who had let her wait in Tru's tent barrel toward her, holding her tan brimmed hat in place.

"So, it was a no?" she hollered.

"Yeah, he was no help at all."

"I told you he wouldn't go for it," she said with smugness, stopping a few feet away from the front of the car.

Danika glanced at the name badge on the short, robust woman in red braids. Stacy Riordan wore the traditional National Park Service green shirt with khakis. "Is he always so bearlike?"

Stacy laughed. "Not always. You just caught him after a survey. Tru's been in the cave for days. He's just hangry."

Danika looked back at the tent and thought about all the footage her camera captured in Dr. Elliot's basement. If there was anyone who could help her identify some of those locations in the photos it would be his Hangry Highness. She thought about going back in and starting over, maybe coming clean about her friendship with Melinda this time. Maybe if he thought there was a connection the two of them shared, he would be more helpful.

But judging by how he was so triggered with her first request, even with a promise of a donation from the trust fund, she had to rethink her approach. Maybe if she brought a little humble pie, it would ease his temper. It wasn't like she hadn't dealt with difficult people before. And giving up so soon really wasn't an option.

She knew she was so close to finding that headdress…not to mention she had promised Brina the King's Palace to keep this job. In less than three weeks there would be a wedding party showing up here. Brina planned to arrive a week early to oversee the preparations. That didn't allow for much time to let the bear calm down.

On a sigh, Danika turned back toward the tent, but before she took two steps, Stacy grabbed her arm and stopped her.

"I like you, Danika," Stacy said. "I'd wait a bit before poking Tru again. But I honestly don't think any amount of time will convince him of bending the rules. The man carries around extra padlocks for when he finds someone has broken into the restricted caves. Keeping people safe is his first priority, and he does a good job with it."

Danika huffed. "Not all the time."

Stacy shrugged and frowned. "Never on purpose though. He takes his job seriously."

Danika brought up the still photos from her SD card on her phone. "Perhaps you can tell me where some of these pictures were taken?"

Stacy hovered close as Danika flipped through each photo of the area. Five pictures in, she stopped Danika with a point to the screen. "That's Slaughter Canyon."

"Slaughter Canyon?" Danika cringed. "Sounds morbid."

The woman's eyebrows wiggled. She smiled. "Don't let the name fool you. Nothing deadly happened there that I know of. It was named for a family who settled there years ago."

Danika waved her phone. "And you're sure this photo was taken there?"

"Absolutely." Stacy pointed at the cliff in the background. "See those markings? Those tell me right there."

Danika went to the next photo. "And this?"

Stacy nodded. "Slaughter Canyon."

Danika swiped for the next and held it up.

"Same. What are you looking for out there? Slaughter Canyon is not open to the public. It's too dangerous to go in there without a guide. We take small groups of experienced cavers in about once a week, but that's it. The rest of the time it's locked up tight."

"Thank you, Stacy. You've been a big help." Danika reached for her SUV door handle, this time with some direction. Dr. Elliot thought Slaughter Canyon was important enough to photograph it numerous times. Would she find more of the missing artifacts hidden away?

"You're not thinking of going out there alone, are you?" Stacy sounded concerned.

Danika opened her door and looked back at the ranger. "It's all part of the job."

"Who knew wedding photography could be so treacherous?"

Danika smirked, letting the woman think that was her sole role. "Thanks for your help." She climbed behind the wheel.

"I have to tell the boss. I hope you know that."

Danika nodded. "I figured as much." Maybe he would escort her, after all.

Or arrest her.

With that, she opened the park map and headed out in the direction of Slaughter Canyon and the caves out there. She drove through the back wilderness area, passing cat's-claw bushes with their curved, sharp-clawed branches that scratched worse than a cat's. Danika had a run-in with some bushes on a cliff climb in Texas. Four years on the University of Texas rock-climbing team gave her a variety of experiences in nature. Landing in the cat's-claw bush was not one of her finer moments.

Danika drove her car as far as she could before the terrain became too rocky. Grabbing her hiking and climbing gear from the hatch just in case, she fitted the side pack in place and opened the photo gallery again. This time she searched through the pictures to find landmarks she needed to look for. After thirty minutes, she finally found her first one.

Excitement bloomed as she searched for more and found them one by one. It was time-consuming, and there had to be a better way.

Then she remembered a photo of a drawing she'd captured from the album. A bunch of squiggly lines that at the time didn't mean anything to her. But perhaps it would now. She swiped fast until the drawing popped up. Initials were scrawled out along the squiggly lines. There was also a circle that was traced three times over itself. Most maps used an *X* to mark the spot. She shrugged and focused on finding her place on the map. The word *knoll* pulled her attention, and she scanned the area for what could be a small hill. Far off, she located something that looked like it fit and headed that way. The direction said to go to the right around it, not over it. As she did, she found a shallow ravine with brush. Using her boot, she pushed aside the branches and realized she almost fell into a hole in the ground.

No, it was a cave.

The opening would barely fit two people, but she sat and lowered herself down into a five-foot drop. From there, she crouched to look into a dark tunnel. Opening her pack, she removed her night-vision goggles and strapped them on, but without a map of the routes down here, she would be lost. Danika gazed longingly down one corridor. Would she find her father's discoveries hidden in here? She took a turn and tripped over something hard.

Down on her hands and knees she went, fumbling to right herself and grabbing on to anything to hold her up. Her hand held something hard and round. Danika peered through the green tinge of her goggles and made out a man's boot beside her hand. She looked to the other side of where she gripped and followed a leg all the way up to the face of a dead man.

Danika released her hold and fell back, only to free-fall to a lower level. She screamed, but her voice stopped short when her body hit the rock floor hard. She winced for a few moments and grit her teeth through the jolt her body just took. She'd fallen before in many of her rock climbs and knew to test her legs and arms to be sure nothing was broken or bruised. Slowly, she pushed up and sought some leverage to pull herself to a standing position.

Her hands shook.

Her hands never shook when she climbed.

But then she'd never come face-to-face with a cadaver on any of her climbs either.

Taking a few deep breaths, Danika reached up to the ledge she'd fallen from and used her hands and arms to push her body up and over to the previous level. She did her best to avoid looking at the body but wondered how he died. After righting herself to a safe position, she dared another glance his way.

A bullet to the front of the head.

A shiver ran up her spine. Her stomach churned with nausea. She moved past him but hit the wall in her attempt to get back to the opening of the cave.

"What are you doing out here?" a distant voice spoke. It sounded like Truman Butler.

The hangry ranger had found her.

She opened her mouth to speak, but only a squeak came out.

"Answer me," Tru spoke again.

"I found a body," she whispered and cleared her throat to try again. "I found a—"

A gunshot blasted from outside, sending the sand spraying all around the cave opening. Danika dropped to the floor of the cave and covered her head. More shots rang out, and a glance upward showed Tru was down on the ground.

She looked up as he looked down into the cave at her. His gun was drawn, and quickly, he scrambled inside, landing beside her. His green eyes were livid. His black hair was covered in sand, as well as the clean T-shirt he had changed into since she saw him in his tent.

"Is he a friend of yours?" Tru asked.

Danika looked back at the body. She tried to shake her head.

"Do you know why he's shooting at me?" He reached for his radio.

Danika glanced back at the opening. It was probably the guy who killed the man down below. But Danika couldn't voice her thoughts, no matter how much she wanted to. All she could do was point downward.

Tru Butler paused with the radio at his lips. His gaze followed the direction she pointed in. He spoke into the radio. "I need patrol out at Slaughter Canyon. Active shooter. Armed and dangerous." He lowered the radio and said, "You're no wedding photographer, are you?"

Tru held his gun at the ready and prayed law enforcement would arrive soon. As a ranger, he could legally carry a firearm, but more often than not, it wasn't used for shoot-outs. The only time he had drawn his weapon to fire was at a rattlesnake about to attack a park visitor. The snake hadn't been firing a gun back.

The woman had yet to answer his question, not that he needed a response. She was obviously not out in these tunnels looking for a place to hold a wedding. He took his eyes off the opening and noticed her petrified expression.

"What are you doing out here?" he demanded in a harsh whisper. He knew he sounded mean, but he wouldn't be half as mean as the sheriff's deputies when they took her in.

Her lips moved in silence.

"What? What do you want to say?" he asked, looking up to watch for anyone coming near the opening. When she still didn't respond, he studied her paled complexion. He wondered if she had hit her head in here somewhere. "Are you hurt?"

Tru knew all about brain injuries. His older brother, Jett, had been in an accident ten years ago and suffered a severe traumatic brain injury that left him with amnesia. He lost all his memories, including those of his loved ones. It destroyed their family and was what sent Tru out of his hometown of Taos. He had been so disconnected and distraught. If he hadn't met Melinda...

Tru shook the direction of his thoughts back to the present. This woman could be hurt. If she had suffered a head injury, she needed help immediately.

"I'm going to get you to the hospital. As soon as backup arrives, I'll help you out of here. I promise." He watched for any sign of understanding.

Nothing.

Tru leaned closer to her face, studying her eyes, the very eyes he thought back in his tent demanded to be explored. Her pupils dilated fine. So no head injury. He snapped his fingers.

She jolted and mumbled, "D-dead b-body."

"Excuse me?"

She pointed behind her, down the hole. "T-there's a dead body d-down there."

"Butler?" someone called to him from outside. "Sheriff's department."

"In the hole!" he hollered back, and a few seconds later a deputy peered inside.

"We got the place surrounded. It's safe to come out. We'll get you back to park headquarters."

"Hold up, Mitch. We might have a body down here."

The woman nodded. "It's right down there. Around the corner. He was shot…in the h-head."

"Let me in to have a look," Mitch said, and Danika moved down to give the officer space. He jumped inside the cave and led the way in the direction she gave. Sure enough, a body lay crumpled on the rock floor just as she'd said. Mitch radioed the secondary scene in as Tru made his way back up to the woman.

He turned the corner, but she was gone. He pulled himself up out of the hole, expecting to see her with the deputies. A scan around showed no evidence that she'd ever existed.

But that wasn't the case. She was very much alive. But if the shooter hadn't been apprehended, then she could be the next one to be shot dead.

THREE

Danika walked in a daze, unsure of where she was going. All she wanted was to get back to her car and regroup…and maybe hide. Where had she gone wrong?

I veered from the plan.

The goal was to investigate the guests of Brina's wedding, with a particular focus on Dr. Elliot. The goal was to find her father's killer and his missing artifacts…and to restore his good name.

When Jared Lewis's body was found, the police determined his death to be a suicide. A single gunshot killed him, and the gun was in his hand. The investigation found him to be destitute with gambling debts still to pay. The news had sent Danika's mother into a deep depression, but Danika refused to believe what the authorities were saying about her dad.

Especially when his artifacts were nowhere to be found.

When she brought this detail to the police, they responded that Jared must have sold it all to pay off his debts.

Case closed.

But it wasn't for Danika, and it never would be until she uncovered the truth of his death and the whereabouts of his life's accomplishments.

With all of her father's old associates all in one place at this wedding, she knew it wouldn't be much longer before the truth was revealed. The guest list would aid her in investigating each of his connections. The clues would direct her next actions in the investigation and bring her another step closer to justice for her father. But instead, her rush to locate the place in the pictures brought her to some other dead body.

A murdered dead body! Murdered in the same way as her father had been.

She rubbed her hands on her pant legs for the tenth time since climbing out of the hole. There wouldn't be enough soap and water to wash away the feeling of touching the body.

How did it end up there? The question burned for an answer. Even if he had been shot, it had to be completely unrelated to her father's death eight years ago.

But Dr. Elliot had a map to the cave. Why would there be a dead man in the same cave?

Maybe this cave had an outlet and was being used to smuggle, and they had no more use for this guy.

Danika stopped cold. Slowly turning around, she faced the expansive Slaughter Canyon and saw how far she'd walked without even realizing it. She could no longer see the sheriff department's Jeeps. She had been directed to sit in the front seat of one, but she must have walked right by it—and mindlessly kept going.

Danika circled around, taking in the high cliffs at her sides. She realized she stood out in the open and felt suddenly exposed. Had the police caught the shooter? She had assumed when they said the area was secured that they had, but what if that wasn't the case? What if she had positioned herself to make Slaughter Canyon live up to its ghastly name?

To Danika's right, she saw the path to Slaughter Canyon. Crossing over rocks and brush, she made her way to the path. Once on it, she felt safer that it was well-worn. That meant people came here often.

But not today.

The rangers opened the cave up once a week for experienced cavers, but that day was not today.

A crunching sound grabbed her attention. It sounded like someone stepped on some small rocks. The hot desert breeze whipped a strand of her hair across her face as she turned to listen for any other sound.

Instead of taking the path back to the visitor center, she stepped backward toward the entry to Slaughter Canyon. Trees covered her, and when she neared the cliff wall with the cave entrance, she crouched low in the shadow of the opening. Unfortunately, the slotted iron gate was padlocked. Its slots were horizontal and wide enough for bats and birds to come and go but not humans.

The feeling of being watched overwhelmed her.

She knew her cell phone had no service out here, but she checked anyway. She turned on her recorder and whispered, "May 15. I saw my first murder victim today. I was also stuck in a cross fire, and I think I'm being followed now. Being a private investigator can be dangerous, and I knew this when I started. I accept whatever happens, and I wouldn't have changed a thing. This story is bigger than my father, and I pray my evidence leads to justice."

She pocketed the phone and took a deep breath. There would be no more hiding in caves.

With that, she stepped out of the shadow of the walls and heard the crack of gunfire.

Tru shot his gun in the air. It was the only thing he could do from a distance of over two hundred feet. There was no way he would get to the man taking aim at the photographer in time to apprehend him.

The gunshot jolted the man enough to look back and lose his sights on his target. The woman also took the moment to start running.

Didn't she know it would only make things worse for herself?

Mitch came running up beside him. "Drop your weapon!" he called out to the man.

Even with two guns pointed on him, the shooter kept his aim on the woman. Mitch shot his weapon in the same moment that the gunman pulled his trigger. Out of the corner of his eye, Tru saw the woman go down, but he barreled toward the shooter at full speed.

Mitch's bullet had hit the man in the leg. He dropped to his knees but still held his gun. "Drop your weapon now!" Tru yelled.

The gunman turned slowly and let the weapon fall. He wore an accomplished smirk as Tru and Mitch approached him carefully. Tru kept his gun raised as Mitch kicked the guy's gun aside and had him widen his legs for arrest.

As Mitch lifted his arms to handcuff him, the guy's smirk turned dangerous toward Tru. His bald head was bright red, and he looked like he enjoyed the fast-food joints a bit too much. His black buttoned short-sleeve shirt hung out of his pants.

"Who are you?" Tru asked.

No answer.

Just before the cuffs clicked into place, the guy leaned to the right and kicked Mitch from behind. He twisted around while reaching down to his ankle.

"Knife!" Tru yelled and barreled toward the man, knocking him down to the ground for Mitch to cuff.

Mitch lifted him up and pushed the man forward from behind. "You're going to regret that."

Two more deputies came running. One said, "We lost the woman."

Tru looked in the direction she had went down…but she was gone. The path she had been on was empty. She had taken off again. "This is park land. I'll get her."

"We want her for questioning," the deputy said, not too happy that she'd left the scene.

Neither was he. And he had his own questions for her.

The wedding photographer, or whatever she was, had a lot of explaining to do. Tru took off as fast as he could to catch up. The woman was strong and quick, and hopefully unhurt. He had endurance to last for weeks in a cave, but his strength came from patience and precision. She was agile with every step she took. She might even have outrun that bullet, or at least dodged it.

Tru picked up his pace and finally spotted the neon orange side pack and white athletic, long-sleeve shirt she wore. He ran faster until he finally came within shouting distance. "Stop running!"

She slowed a bit to look over her shoulder.

"Please," he said, getting winded. "The shooter is apprehended. You're safe now."

Her feet slowed and came to a stop, but she stayed back from him, a wary expression on her face. "I'm definitely not safe."

He approached her as he would a wounded animal. "Why do you say that?"

"Because I know you're about to turn me into the police, and when certain people see I've been arrested, everything will be ruined."

"Like what?"

She dropped her gaze to her hiking boots. "Like years of hard work."

He didn't think she was talking about taking pictures, but she had yet to come clean with him. "They just want you to come in for questioning. If you haven't done anything wrong, they won't arrest you."

She looked at him. "I have nothing to say to them."

"They're gonna want to know why you were out here."

She shrugged. "I was looking for something. Something that belonged to my father."

Now they were getting somewhere. "He left it in the cave?"

She frowned. "Someone stole it from him. I have a valid reason to believe it's stashed somewhere out here." She nodded in the direction behind him. "The dead guy and the shooter only confirm it."

Tru took a moment and considered her words. They made sense. But he wasn't an investigator. "Come with me and share your story with the detective. Perhaps when he hears he'll be helpful."

She sighed but walked toward him. As she passed by him, she mumbled, "Or he'll say I had motive to murder."

Tru followed the woman from behind without another word. He couldn't say she was wrong. But he also couldn't say she was innocent. It was best to let the law take it from here so he could get back to work. He had a cave to explore and map.

But perhaps that would make him the best person to help her. As an expert caver, he could easily explore the cave to search for what she was looking for.

He shook his head. He wouldn't let a pretty face make him break protocol. Been there, done that, and the last woman didn't live to tell about it.

FOUR

Danika sat in a chair at park headquarters. Tru's office consisted of the desk with three chairs around it and bookshelves behind it. As she sat alone waiting for him to return with the investigator, she took in things he thought worthy enough to showcase on his shelves. Various rocks and bones were placed in between textbooks on geology and archaeology. She should have felt nervous waiting for this interview to take place, but surprisingly his possessions gave her a sense of peace. If she blotted out the rest of the day's happenings, she could almost envision herself sitting in her father's office. He too displayed his findings and sources of knowledge. After he died, she pored over everything of his in the hopes he'd left her a clue. The only thing different between the possessions of Jared Lewis and Truman Butler were the absence of pictures on Tru's shelves. Where her father had displayed photographs of his friends and loved ones, Tru appeared to have no connection to any other human being. For a moment, Danika pitied the man. But then she rationalized that he didn't even have a picture of the woman he was supposed to marry, and her pity turned to resentment.

She moved her gaze away from his possessions to find his PhD and various diplomas and certificates on the wall. He apparently had done a lot in his thirty years. She knew he had studied for his doctorate at the same school she and her friend Melinda had attended. Danika remembered her senior year and how Melinda became infatuated with this older student. As far as Melinda was concerned, this man hung the moon, and she would follow him wherever he led.

Even right to her death.

Danika curled her hands around the armrest of the wooden chair and took a deep breath as the door behind her opened. The two men she was waiting for talked about some other matter that had to do with the excavation, she supposed. The investigator came and sat beside her while Tru went around the other side of his desk and took his chair directly across from her.

"Did I say something wrong?" Tru asked. "You look ready to maim someone."

Danika bit her tongue and shook her head. "I'll be fine. Let's just get this over with." She turned to face the investigator, who she assumed was a plainclothes officer from the sheriff's department. "Detective?"

The man with short blond hair and large biceps extended his strong hand for her to shake. He looked ex-military. Offering a slanted smile, he said, "I'm Bard Holland. You can just call me Bard. I'm an investigator for the Bureau of Land Management. The cave you happened upon is on our land jurisdiction, so I'll be taking over the investigation from here. Can I ask what led you to this off-limits cave?"

Danika glanced back at Tru. "I asked for a guide, but I was turned down."

Tru scoffed. "I wouldn't have taken you in there anyway, guide or not. No guide would have."

"Well, then, it's a good thing I took matters into my own hands. Who knows how long that guy would've been down there."

Tru leaned forward and placed his forearms on his desk. "None of this is good. There are locks on these caves to protect people, even people who think they are doing a good thing." He studied her face, paying close attention to her eyes. "I'm still not convinced you weren't hurt in there. Am I right?"

Danika dropped her gaze to her lap and brought her hands to fold there. She didn't want to tell him that she'd fallen. It may have been a short fall, but it was a fall, nonetheless.

He leaned back and nodded. "Just as I thought. You'll be going to first aid after this."

Now Danika scoffed. "You won't tell me what to do. You are not my lead."

Tru tilted his head and squinted his eyes. "You're a climber?"

Danika realized her choice of words had given her away. In climbing, groups would divide up into twos. There was the lead and there was the second, and together they made it to the top of the wall or cliff. Melinda had been her lead.

"I was in college. Now I just do it for sport." Danika braced herself for his next question. Would it lead to his realization of who she was?

"What school?"

She smirked and looked at his diploma. "University of Texas, San Antonio."

She could practically see the wheels turning in his head as he tried to place her. The rock-climbing team wasn't that big. She figured it wouldn't be long before he put two and two together.

Tru cleared his throat and looked to the investigator. "Bard, why don't you go ahead and start your questions. I'll save mine for after. Yours are more pertinent for the crime at hand, I'm sure." He glanced her way with a look that said they weren't finished yet.

Bard studied the two of them but quickly shook his head and began his line of questioning. "Did you know the deceased or the shooter?"

"No. " Danika folded her hands in her lap.

"Did you overhear any conversation that might allude to why they were there?"

"No."

"Did the shooter say anything to you at any point?"

She unfolded her hands and leaned forward. "I keep telling you I don't know anything. I didn't know anyone, and I can't be of any help to you. I was literally in the wrong place at the wrong time." That part wasn't true. Danika was pretty sure she was in the exact place she needed to be, just at the wrong time.

"Does this mean you have no plans to return there?" Tru asked. "Because if you do, I do need to warn you that you're trespassing. That is a restricted cave, and you're not allowed to be in there."

Danika nodded. "I understand." His piercing eyes told her he didn't believe her. She looked back at Bard. "I really wish I could help you, but I just happened upon this man and know nothing about him or the shooter. I came looking for a certain cave and I thought I had found it.

There was no lock on it, and I would have fallen in had I not been looking. Someone else unlocked that cave. It wasn't me. I know now not to go into the restricted caves alone. Next time, I will have a guide." She avoided Tru's glare but felt it singeing the tips of her hair. She let him know she would be returning, no matter what.

Bard handed her his card, with the letters *BLM* on the corner for Bureau of Land Management. Since he was a federal agent, she nearly spilled her idea of her father's artifacts being stolen, but quickly reined in that desire. She'd been down this road with law enforcement before and it led to nowhere. They were convinced Jared Lewis had died by suicide, and nothing she said would change that. Her insistence only provoked ridicule. The next time she confided in law enforcement of any kind, she would have the proof she needed to back it up, and no one would be dismissive of her again.

Danika tucked the card into her pants pocket. Perhaps, when she found her father's collection, she would call up Bard and get him involved in the recovery and redistribution to the rightful owners.

"If you think of anything else that might give us a clue of what these men were doing out there, please call, day or night. That's my personal number, which I don't give out very often. Tru's my friend, so I'll give it to you." Bard looked at Tru and back at Danika. "I get the feeling there's some history between the two of you, and I do hope you'll work that out. Go easy on Tru. Some people keep digging even if what they're looking for is staring right back at them."

Both Danika and Tru scoffed at the same time.

Bard laughed and stood. "With that, I'll take my leave. I'm off to the hospital to see if the shooter is ready to talk. Tru, I'll be in touch with any information that you might need for the park. Let's hope this was a fluke and not some operation going on under our noses." He headed to the door for a final nod before departing.

Once the door clicked closed, Danika kept her gaze to her lap. She wished she could have followed Bard out, but her work here wasn't done yet. And whether she liked it or not, she needed Tru Butler's assistance.

"Now that you've told Bard everything you don't know—" Tru leaned back in his chair and folded his hands at his chest "—why don't you start telling me what you do know."

Danika studied his annoyingly condescending expression. More than anything she wanted to walk out of this room and never look back.

She leaned forward and lifted her chin, placing her arms on his desk. "There is an operation going on right under your nose. Ancient Native American artifacts are being smuggled and hidden in these caves. Millions of dollars' worth, and more than one person has died because of it."

Tru pressed his lips tight and took a few breaths. She watched his chest rise and fall three times before he opened his mouth and said, "Who are you? And don't tell me you're some wedding photographer."

"I'm a private investigator, and I need a guide. Will you help me or not?"

Tru burst out laughing. When he tried to speak, he sputtered. "You're a PI?" He laughed again.

Danika did not.

Slowly, he sobered and leaned back into his chair again. "Oh, you're serious. Okay." He nodded as he processed this information. This woman was full of surprises, and none of them good. He leaned forward and put his arms on his desk. "So, you're a private investigator. Why not tell Bard? Perhaps the two of you could have teamed up to solve this case." He nearly laughed again, but the flaming daggers in her eyes made him think better of it.

"I'm thinking about it. I have his card if I should change my mind, or if I should need assistance. Right now, in this moment, the only assistance I need is a guide."

Tru shook his head. "You're too much of a high risk. You've already proven that by dropping down into that cave. Do you even know how deep that goes? Or how far? Any farther past that dead guy and you would've dropped 150 feet in the pitch black. The cave extends for miles."

She leaned forward. "Whose land does it come out on?" Determination and inquisitiveness was a becoming expression on her, and before he came to his senses, he nearly told her.

"So you can jump into your little SUV and drive right over there? I don't think so."

She shrugged and stood. "You can withhold information from me all you want, Mr. Butler, but it will not stop me from finding out in other ways." She turned briskly and headed for the door.

"What part of no don't you understand?"

She slipped out without another word.

He nearly brought his fist down on his desk. Looking down at his hand he saw he had crumpled up his recent notes from his survey. His cell phone rang beside him, and he let go of the paper.

Caller ID read Luci Butler.

Tru let a deep sigh go and took another deep breath before answering his sister's call. "What's up, squirt?"

"You didn't call me You know you're supposed to call me as soon as you come out of the caves. That was our deal."

A smile spread on Tru's face and he relaxed in his chair as he imagined his little sister, who was four years younger than him, her pixie-cut black hair and lashes so long they fluttered like a butterfly. She barely reached five feet and bounced around through life just like one as well. When their older brother lost his memories ten years ago, the two of them became closer than ever before. Where once he and Jett were inseparable as they trekked through the mountains of Taos, now Luci was his extra appendage, even with her living so far away in Santa Fe.

"I'm sorry. I've had a rough day."

She scoffed. "That's what you always say. Every day is a rough day with you."

Tru didn't want to worry her, yet it wasn't so often that he got to say, "I was too busy being shot at. There, how's that for rough?"

Silence filtered through the phone.

Luci whispered, "Please tell me you're joking."

"No joke, Luce." He cleared his throat and explained to her about the guy in the cave and how he helped apprehend the shooter.

"But not before he took a shot at you."

"Yeah." Tru decided it best not to tell her that it

was more than one. It was over and there was no sense making her more worried. "But he's been arrested now. He was wounded so he's at the hospital. He'll head to jail after he's stable. Nothing to worry about, squirt."

"You always tell me not to worry, and I know we're not supposed to worry about anything. God tells us that over and over again, but…" Her voice trailed off, and Tru knew what she was thinking.

"But Jett," he finished for her.

"Yeah." Her voice cracked in her response. "I know all will turn to good, and has, but I still remember the pain of losing the brother I knew and loved. I don't want to go through that again. Please tell me you'll be careful. I didn't think being a ranger would be this dangerous."

Tru reached for his gun at his side. "Crime can happen anywhere. Sometimes you don't even have to go looking for it." He gazed at the door that Danika had left through moments before. "And sometimes you do." He let go of his gun and brought his hand to his forehead, thinking he had to be a fool to go after her again.

But there was something about her that he couldn't place. Something that made him feel responsible for her. It was almost like he…knew her from somewhere, that they were connected in some way that went beyond the day's events. Maybe he knew her from school? She was on the rock-climbing team. Perhaps Melinda knew her…

Another call came in. A glance down at his phone and he could see it was Bard.

"Luci, I have to go. Official business calls."

"Wait, are you coming to my Memorial Day picnic? You're the only one who hasn't responded."

The phone beeped again. Tru hesitated in answering Luci. If he had his way, it would be an automatic no. He hadn't seen his family since Christmas. *Awkward* didn't completely describe it. Luci wanted to forget how their family imploded, but no matter how much he tried, he couldn't.

"I'll have to get back to you." He cut off and clicked over to the other line without a goodbye. "What's up, Bard?"

"Butler, the guy is dead."

Tru squinted at his phone. "Of course he's dead. He took a bullet to his head. He was stone-cold."

"No, not him. The shooter. I got to the hospital. He made it through surgery and was in a room recuperating. I went in to talk to him and found him dead. It doesn't look natural."

Tru stood from his chair, crashing it against the bookshelves behind him. "Mitch hit his leg. There's no way that shot—"

"Superficial. He's not to blame."

"Well, then…"

"Someone got to him in his hospital room, while under guard, mind you. Someone shut him up and made sure he couldn't sing."

Tru glanced at the door again, thinking about what Danika said about a smuggling ring. Was the PI onto something? If so, would someone shut her up next?

"Bard, I need to do some digging. I'll let you know what I find out."

"Anything to do with that pretty hiker?"

"She definitely knows more than she's saying."

"Then don't trust her."

FIVE

Danika flipped through the books in the Carlsbad Caverns bookstore early the next morning. She'd chosen a few trail maps on obscure caves that the general public typically avoided and started to plan her day of exploring. She opened one book written by a caver who shared about his extreme excursions. He told a story about one off-trail tour where after a three-to-four-hour trek of crawling through tight enclosures, he entered into an immense carved-out cavern with a gigantic formation dubbed the Hall of the White Giant. She slammed the book shut and questioned her intelligence at thinking she could find her father's artifacts in such an enormous place. She was taking on a giant herself. It would require years to go through the network of this underworld. And these were 119 caves on park property. There was so much more to explore past the boundaries. Just how many of them extended out into non-park property?

Her train of thought led her to open the maps again. Perhaps she shouldn't be looking at the caves that had openings on both sides within the park. The caves that opened outside the park property would make successful smuggling routes. Artifacts could go from protected federal property and disappear in the night through a dark underworld grid of rock and worm-holes.

Danika shivered at the thought. She had no fear of heights, but tight spaces were another thing altogether. She dropped the map into her handcart to buy, but as soon as she turned toward the checkout, she bumped into a person standing there.

Air whooshed from her lungs as she came into con-tact with his hard barrel chest. She looked up to apol-ogize, but he quickly turned around and headed for the exit. "I'm sorry," she called out. The man didn't acknowledge her.

Before he made it to the doorway, she took in his salt-and-pepper thick head of hair from the back. He wore a yellow, button-down plaid shirt, untucked and hanging down over his black jeans, and black trail shoes. She noticed them splattered with dirt. That fact she shook off. Everyone hiking through these trails came out with splattered shoes. She did wonder though at his fast retreat…and why he had been stand-ing so close to her to begin with. Had he been glanc-ing over her shoulder to see what she was looking at? It could've been something as innocent as curiosity. But then why not just say that?

Danika rushed to the counter and quickly bought her items. She threw the cash down on the counter and said, "Keep the change for a donation." She grabbed up her maps and books and exited the store. A glance to her left and right didn't reveal the direction he went.

Then she looked to her right again. She thought she saw the flutter of his loose shirt as he took a turn at the end of the hall. She headed that way in a near run through the crowd. When she broke through the cluster of people, she picked up her steps and raced to the corner...and stopped at the sight of Brina coming her way.

"Danika? What are you doing here?" Brina neared her, dressed in fashionable tan pants and a crisp white blouse. She wore a tan brimmed hat on her back with a string that rested below her neck. She looked ready for a photo shoot in a safari Jeep that wouldn't actually go anywhere.

Stunned, it took Danika a moment to respond. "What are *you* doing here?"

Brina huffed. Looking over her shoulder, she nodded to someone coming up behind her, but Danika only looked for the man in the yellow shirt. "We came to check the King's Palace out. After all, we'll be having our wedding there in a few weeks. Thanks to you!" Brina beamed with excitement. "Terrence and I are so thankful to you for such a wonderful gift."

Danika gave up her quest for the man who had been standing so close to her and focused on Terrence coming toward her.

Terrence *and* Dr. Martin Elliot.

"You're all here," Danika stated the obvious in her concern. "The wedding won't happen for three weeks. You drove six hours just to check the place out?"

Brina laughed. "Of course not. We flew. We can't waste another day. There is so much to do now that the location will be different. I may have to change the flowers as well as the guest list."

Danika's heart leaped. "Why would you change the guest list?" She glanced at Dr. Elliot then back at his daughter.

Brina shrugged a slim shoulder. "I don't want to be crammed in. It needs to feel natural and if that means some people are not invited then so be it."

"But haven't the invites already gone out?" Danika had researched every single person on that list. If only a fraction of them would be attending now her investigation could be disrupted. "Perhaps I can do a video stream and some people can be watching from the amphitheater."

Brina clapped once and gasped. "That sounds perfect." She turned to her father. "Would this make you happy?" Brina glanced back at Danika. "He was not happy with my decision of cutting the list."

Danika observed Dr. Elliot's aloof stance. He stood five feet away from his daughter and soon-to-be son-in-law, but his attire wasn't as neatly crisp as his daughter's. Sadly, his manner of dress reminded her of her own father's. Her dad was always ready for an impromptu dig. His loose white linen shirts very rarely saw an iron. His cargo pants always held some kind of tool he had yet to return to its place. Danika glanced down at Dr. Elliot's pants and wondered if he too carried a shovel or pick or brush like her dad always had. She found herself softening toward the man, but quickly reined that direction of thought under control. This man had her father's blood on his hands, no matter how similarly they dressed. She just needed to figure out how he pulled off such an elaborate crime.

He couldn't have done it alone, and someone on the guest list was the key to unravel how he did it.

Terrence laughed. "You would think he would be happy with cutting the guest list and cutting the ticket price of this event." He draped his arm around his fiancée and squeezed her shoulder. Danika noticed how Brina melted into his embrace and gave him a soft smile.

Perhaps their relationship was a true love match.

Danika had just assumed this was another business transaction that their fathers had put together, but judging by their affection for each other, that might not be the case.

Terrence Lindsay was ten years older than Brina and the son of Dr. Elliot's financier, Derral Lindsay. Terrence had taken the oil route for his career instead of his father's finance world. A little digging on Danika's part had shown there was some animosity between father and son, as his father considered himself an environmentalist and preservationist of the land and his son was going around Texas digging up oil wells. It apparently was a major blot on the family's image. Danika had just assumed this marriage was a way to correct the blemish Terrence had caused the family. But the way Brina and he held hands and looked at each other with adoration said otherwise.

"But I love your idea of a video stream," Terrence said. "Now I know why you came so highly recommended. You're quick on your feet. I like that." He flashed her a grin of perfect white teeth all lined up in a row. Danika wondered if he had been married before and mentally filed that question away for later. For now, she needed to get them out of there.

"Well, since that's taken care of, I'm sorry you came all this way for something we could have done on a phone call. Next time, just call me and we can discuss the layout." Danika started to guide them back toward the exit.

Sabrina pushed back. "We still want to see the cave. It's been years since I've been in it. Perhaps we can get someone to escort us to the King's Palace. Can you ask the friend you know who works here? The one who approved our wedding?"

"Excuse me? What wedding?" The voice of Tru Butler spoke from behind Danika. She did everything she could to keep her smile plastered on her face as she turned to face him head-on. Tru looked disheveled since she saw him last, like he had slept in his office.

She ignored his mussed hair and dropped her gaze to his badge on his chest. "You know, the one we talked about." She urged him with her eyes to go along with her. Though why she expected him to was beyond her. But she still had to try…and hope he would come through. "You're so funny, Tru. Always the kidder." She lightly punched him in the arm as if they were old friends. "Don't give this bride and groom a heart attack, *please*?"

Something wasn't adding up. Tru glanced past the people standing in front of him, his gaze targeting the exit doors behind them before zeroing in on Danika's pleading expression. He registered that she wanted him to go along with her idea of a wedding event in the main cavern, but all he could think about was how grateful he was that he had found her still alive. He needed to know where she was staying, not that a guard would help. The shooter had also been under guard at the hospital and was still killed. Tru figured he needed to consider everyone, even the park employees, suspect.

"Tru?" The bride stepped up beside Danika and extended her hand. "I'm Sabrina Elliot. I'm delighted to be able to hold our wedding in the cavern. Thank you for making it possible. We're here to work on the details and would like to go down into the cavern to scope out the layout. If you're free to join us that would be fabulous. But I understand if you're not right now. Perhaps tomorrow we can sit down and go over our ideas?"

"Yes, tomorrow," Danika said and looped her arm through his. "Tru just emerged from an extended trek through one of the caves and has a lot of work to catch up on. Isn't that right, Tru?" She patted his hand, pulling his attention back to the nonsensical conversation. He tried to focus but thoughts of possibly closing the park with a killer on the loose took precedence. Should he tell these people to go back and find a safer place to get married? After all he had done to make sure Carlsbad Caverns was as safe as possible, he hated to say such a thing.

But two men had been murdered on his watch.

And Danika's knowledge of why made her the next target. If anyone should be going back where they came from, it should be her. But it was probably too late for that, not that he believed she would.

Tru forced a smile and looked to the couple and the older man beside them. "Tomorrow would be great. Let's say around ten in the morning. If you all don't mind, I need to speak to Danika about some other matters here at the park…some, uh, photos she's taking for us."

Brina's eyes widened. "Oh, interesting. Shall we meet at the cave, then?"

"Yes." He guided Danika toward his office. "See you tomorrow. And congratulations," he said as an afterthought, then left the group.

"I can explain," Danika said under her breath as they moved away from eavesdroppers.

"You'll be doing a lot of that in a moment," he muttered softly.

"I needed to promise Brina that I could get her the cavern for the wedding, or she was going to fire me. Thank you for agreeing to this."

"I haven't agreed to anything, and I wasn't talking about the wedding. The shooter is dead. Murdered in his hospital room. You're going to start telling me everything you know, so I can determine if park guests are in danger. Including you."

"Me? Why would I be in danger?"

"Because in your investigating, you put a target on your back." He guided her through the thickening crowd. They passed the bookstore, filled with people excited to head down into the caverns and having no idea that dangerous people were on the loose around them. Tru had spent the last four years making sure the caves were safe. He had been meticulous in knowing every drop or uneven surface within them, but he'd neglected to reinforce the security from outside.

"Thank you for not blowing my cover with Brina and Dr. Elliot," Danika said after a few moments of walking in silence.

He reached his office and realized the door was left open. He barely registered what she was saying to him. Then heard the word *cover.* "You're undercover as a photographer," he stated as he put all the details about this woman together. "That's how this wedding fits in. You're working a case that involves those people," he said under his breath.

She moved to enter his office, but he put his arm up to stop her. With the shake of his head and nod to have her go behind him, he pushed the door all the way open and scanned the room. He tried to remember if he had closed it and carefully stepped inside. A check behind his desk came up empty. Nothing seemed touched by any other hands but his. He returned to the door and closed it, directing Danika to have a seat.

"We need to talk about the possible danger you're in. I have to be honest, I feared someone might've already tracked you down. I'm hoping they'll just think of you as an innocent person in the wrong place at the wrong time. Maybe just leave you alone because you don't know anything." Tru took his seat around the other side of the desk and stared out his window at the packed parking lot of the visitor center. It was springtime, mid-May, and families traveled from far and wide to visit their nation's parks. He looked back at Danika, a plan forming. "I want you to stick close to me and see if this dies down. Give it a couple days.

If we don't see anyone lurking, or some suspicious behavior, then you could be just fine to go on your way."

She pressed her lips tight. "Who made you the lead in all this? You should know something right now. I am no one's second." .

A heavy silence settled between them. This was the second time she gave reference to rock climbing. When climbing in pairs, the lead climber prepared the way for the one to come behind him or her. The second followed, removing the reinforcement tools that allowed for a safe climb. The second depended on the lead to have secured those reinforcements correctly the first time. Being the lead came with responsibility.

Or people died.

Tru closed his eyes on the memory of Melinda's scream. The sound would stay with him forever and woke him up many nights. All because a reinforcement hadn't been secure. Now he double- and triple-checked everything.

"Well, then, we have a problem because I am no one's second either. And honestly I don't even like having one."

SIX

Danika needed a guide. She had a bag full of maps, but nothing came even close to having a living, breathing expert with her as she set out on this course and down into these holes. It could take her weeks before she found a match to the photo of the map she had on her phone. Tru could probably look at it and know within moments.

But it meant humbling herself. It meant trusting the man who had taken Melinda away from her...permanently. What if he led her to her own death as well? But what if she led him to his? Tru needed to be able to trust her skills too.

"We need a problem," she said.

Tru huffed in her direction. He leaned forward and placed his hands on his desk. "Excuse me? You don't consider this a problem? You need *another* one? Danika, your life is at risk."

"Taking risks has never scared me. And I meant we need a problem, as in a boulder. I need a guide I can trust, but you also need to know I can hold my own. Until then we're at an impasse. You know the area better than I do. Take your pick of boulders and lead the way."

Danika kept her body straight in the chair as she waited for his response. His hesitancy spoke loudly of his concern that he may not be the best leader. She waited for him to admit that.

"I have just the place," he said instead. A smug expression morphed onto his face. The battle of wits and strength lay between them. "But first, what has been your climbing level in the past? I want to be sure it won't be too difficult for you."

Danika laughed. Little did he know she had been climbing over things her whole life. From the moment she climbed out of her crib at a year old to the excavation sites she climbed up while her father painstakingly unearthed them. "My last two climbs have been V11 and V12 problems." In the rock-climbing world, boulders were called problems. "But I have successfully solved a V14."

Tru's eyes widened, and it gave her a little delight in proving her skill. "Where was the V14?"

"I climbed Golden Shadow in Rocklands, South Africa. It was one of a few international climbs my team in college did."

Tru's face paled in a matter of seconds. His eyes drifted to the drawer at his right. Slowly he reached for it and paused with a shaking hand. Something told Danika that whatever was in that drawer would force them both to admit the history the two of them had. Or rather the connection they had.

Melinda had been on that trip.

Tru would know Melinda had also solved that problem. Very few women in the world had. It was a climb that featured difficult, tension-dependent moves that suspended a climber upside down and sometimes hanging from one hand. One wrong move would send the climber to the rock floor. It was a solo climb, but it had been Melinda who solved the problem first. She had a way of computing every crevice and ledge and taking the boulder under her possession. It was what made her a great lead and partner.

He opened the drawer and withdrew a framed photo, which he placed on the desk between them. "You knew her."

It wasn't a question. Tru was putting the details of the problem in front of him together as quickly as Melinda mapped out that South African boulder.

Danika glanced down at the picture and felt the tears always so close and ready to spill when she thought of her friend. It was still so hard to believe she was gone. There was no sense in denying it. Danika was pretty sure it was written all over her face.

"That's how I know you," Tru said. "Our paths must've crossed at a climb, or when I picked…when I picked her up after practice sometimes. I knew you from somewhere. I assume you tracked me down because you also remember me."

Danika bit her tongue to keep from accusing him of taking away her partner. That was one part of the puzzle that he didn't know. And it was the only one that mattered to her. "I vaguely remember you, but yes, I had hoped you would recognize me and would want to help me with this case. When you hadn't, I didn't push it." She looked back at her beautiful friend's smile, frozen in place for the rest of time. Danika was glad to see he wasn't as cold as his office portrayed. He did have a photo, even if it wasn't displayed at the moment.

But that didn't mean she trusted him. She would hold that judgment until after the climb.

"I have my equipment in my car. Shall I grab it?" she said, composing herself quickly and standing.

Tru stood and walked toward his closet. "We can use mine. I'll drive." In a matter of moments, he had his backpack of gear and was leading her to the exit and out through a back entrance to the employee parking lot. He drove a black Jeep with some mud splatter up on the rims. However, the interior was void of anything personal. Not even a gum wrapper or empty coffee cup was in the holder. It reminded her of his office with a seemingly untouched feel to it.

"Is this a new car for you?" she asked.

He shrugged from behind the wheel as they headed out of the parking lot and out onto the desert highway. "I typically drive my work vehicle, why?"

"You leave no trace of yourself behind."

He smiled. "Nope. That's the plan. I tend to be a minimalistic individual, if you haven't noticed."

"I've noticed."

Tru drove for a while in silence before saying, "I suppose my lifestyle calls for an awareness of my surroundings and what I might leave behind. I spend most of my time in caves, where I have to carry all of my trash out. Nothing can be left behind."

Tru flashed a wide grin of beautiful teeth and an even more captivating dimple she didn't know he had.

When he smiled, Danika could see what Melinda saw in him.

The thought sobered her, and she faced forward, stunned at thinking such a thing. A handsome face didn't discount his poor decisions in putting her friend in harm's way.

"Anyway," she said in an attempt to return to the subject, "with climbing I don't usually have to worry about that, unless it's a multiple-day track. Most of my climbs are single boulders to overcome. I hope that's what you're taking me to now."

Tru nodded. "The place I'm bringing you to is very similar to what you might find in a cave. You want to test my skills as a lead, but I also need to be sure you can handle the terrain of the underground."

"I assure you I can."

He reached into his pocket and removed something. He passed it over to her, and as she took it from him, she realized it was a handkerchief. "What's this for?"

"It's a blindfold. In the caves, you don't get to look at the full problem that you're about to climb. The cloth is porous so you'll see a bit of what's in front of you, just like a cave. But that's it." He turned onto a dirt road, and the Jeep began to tremble over the rocks. Ahead she could see the cluster of boulders, knowing one of them awaited her. Just moments ago, she had no concern of taking them on.

That was before she knew that she would have to climb it blind.

Tru expected Danika to back out. He parked his Jeep on the side of the road and led the way to the smaller of the three boulders. He wouldn't put her life in jeopardy by leading her to the largest one, and he was only joking about the blindfold. He expected her to balk, but surprisingly she took it in stride. He didn't know if that was a testament to her skill or not, but he would find out in a moment how agile she was on the rocks. He would see her skill right away and know if he could take her into the deepest wormholes and highest drop-offs that the sun never reached.

Tru removed the backpack from his shoulder and unzipped it. Inside were his reinforced ropes and anchors. He passed over a bag of chalk for her to prepare her hands to keep them from slipping on the rocks. As she clapped her hands, sending a puff of chalk into the air, he watched her study the surface of the boulder intently. He wasn't much of a rock climber, and typically depended on harnesses and repelling than maneuvering on the surface of the boulder.

"What are you doing?" he asked as he removed his ropes from the bag.

"Mapping my way up," she replied without looking at him. "Very rarely is the assent straight up. Some divots will hold my toes, while some others will give my hands something to cup or to hang from."

He handed her the ropes. "How about you just hang from these."

She turned to him for the first time and looked at the ropes in his hands. "They're split." She took them from him and showed where the ropes were not secure.

Tru studied his ropes in shock. "This makes no sense. These are rarely used. Most of the caves have ropes anchored that remain there. When I used them last they were fine."

Danika shrugged. "I'm not using them now. Besides, I trust myself more than I do a rope." She headed toward the boulder.

"Wait. Are you telling me you're going up without any support? I don't think that's wise."

She looked back at him. "I can handle it."

Then she put the blindfold on.

Tru dropped the backpack and stepped forward. "I wasn't serious about the blindfold. Please don't do it." He made a reach for her, but she turned away from him and ran straight at the boulder. When she was about ten feet away she took a leap into the air and jammed her foot into one of those divots she had mentioned. Her hand latched on to some crevice above but only for a moment. She bounced the foot to give her momentum to leap up to a higher foothold and to another crevice. Three more times she did this until she was three quarters the way up to the top.

Then she stopped.

Tru moved to stand below her just in case she fell. His heart felt like it was lodged in his throat. He didn't think he had taken a breath since she made that first leap. "Danika, you don't have to do this. It's obvious you know what you're doing. I'm supposed to be leading you. Please let me do that. Please don't go any higher."

"Shhh," she said. "Let me think."

"At least take the blindfold off." He held his arms wide and locked his legs. At any second, he expected her to fall back. She had to be about fifteen feet off the ground with only five feet left to go.

She reached her right arm out, felt the rock, patting until she found what she was looking for, and latched on. Her left hand reached over her right hand where it was placed and found another spot to hold on to. With both hands holding tight, she lifted her feet off the small ledges they were on and turned her body vertical. Only her upper body strength held her up. Her muscles flexed and shook, but her hold was secure.

Then one of her feet found the higher ledge and she jammed her foot into it and used it as a lever to jettison her up and over the top of the rock.

Danika let out a loud whoop and tore the handkerchief from her eyes in victory. She lifted both her arms to the sky and beamed as bright as the sun shining behind her. A desert breeze filtered in and whipped her long ponytail across her face. Even still, she appeared onc with the rock landscape around her, strong and bold.

"All right, Lewis. You have what it takes," Tru called up to her and smiled.

She looked down and pointed at the boulder. "But do you?" She dared him with her words. "I should know too before I follow you into a cave."

Tru looked at his damaged climbing gear and realized he had never climbed without it. "To be honest, I'm not so sure I could go solo. I think the victory in this one goes to you."

He expected her to give another shout of joy, but instead she looked behind her and her smile faltered. "Is something wrong?" he called up. At the top of the boulder was a plateau that went for miles. Nothing but crackled dry beds of sand, mesquite bushes and the occasional tumbleweed. But perhaps she saw some animal. "Danika?" he shouted when she disappeared from his view.

Tru took a step forward but stopped with no plan of how to get to her. He moved back to try to see her again.

A scream broke through the desolate desert.

"Danika!" Tru had no choice now but to go up, even without protective gear. He raced forward and took the same leap she had, finding the crevice to land on. His hands gripped frantically for something to hold on to as he felt himself falling.

Then nothing but air flew past him as he fell to the ground on his back.

Tru groaned at the impact, but he knew he couldn't stay down. He pushed himself up to stand as he recollected the direction Danika had taken up the rock. He pulled every memory of her movements from his mind. He stepped back to give himself the running space again. But this time he knew exactly where his hands had to go.

As he ran and threw himself into the air, he realized Danika's life was similar to his own. He may chart caves to map them, but she charted boulders and mapped her way to the top. He sought out the places she had charted before him. He couldn't believe she did this blindfolded. His muscles shook as he held his body still. He looked up and thought how much larger the boulder looked from this point of view. From below he hadn't thought it was that big. Hanging on the side told him otherwise. He didn't dare look below him. He just might give up. But he couldn't, not when Danika was in jeopardy.

Perhaps a coyote attacked her? He doubted a big-horn sheep would.

Then he thought of his damaged climbing gear. No, not damaged.

Sabotaged.

But how? When?

As Tru hung from the side of the boulder, he remembered the open door to his office. He had shut it but never locked it. When he returned it was wide-open. Whoever did this, must've been in the process of destroying his climbing gear and heard him returning with Danika. The intruder must have had just enough time to get out of the room but left the door open in his or her wake.

Were they now on top of this boulder with Danika? Had he sent her up here only to be a third victim? The idea blinded him with guilt when he needed his vision more than anything to reach her.

Tru squeezed his eyes and pictured Danika at this portion of her climb. He took the next steps up and remembered how she had to turn her body sideways to reach the next level and push herself up and over. With every ounce of strength in him he began to do the same maneuver. He twisted his body sideways and let his left foot swing to that ledge. He missed it twice. His arms trembled with exertion. Sweat poured from his temples into his eyes, blinding him just as she had been. He could see only what he felt. He realized this is how she climbed as well. She felt her way up the boulder and solved the problem. His third attempt made the connection with the ledge and, just as she had done, put all his weight on it and used it as the catalyst with the last bit of his strength to push himself up and over the top.

His body landed hard, sending a puff of dry sand into his already blurred vision. He swiped at his eyes with his trembling hands and cleared enough to see she was nowhere in sight. He attempted to push himself up but only fell flat on his face again. His muscles were exhausted. He scanned the horizon of the wide-open sky with nothing but red-and-brown terrain for miles.

And no sight of Danika Lewis in any direction.

He pushed himself up and swiped at his eyes again to see clearer. Then he noticed blood on the ground. He rushed over and saw that two tracks extended past the blood, as if someone was being dragged.

But to where?

And those tracks didn't look like an animal had taken her. They were large footprints of a human's boot.

The killer?

Tru couldn't help but think he had just led another woman to her death.

SEVEN

Danika groaned in a semiconscious state. She opened her eyes, but the blinding light of the afternoon sun caused her head to ache. She quickly closed them again and took a moment to figure out what happened. She remembered being proud of her accomplishment of climbing the boulder solo, but then a noise behind her had caught her attention from...from Tru.

"Tru," she mumbled. Where was he? The last she had seen of him, he had been down below.

And then someone had grabbed her from behind.

Danika jolted in panic and tried to sit up but couldn't. She quickly realized something confined her. Her arms were bound to her sides. She forced her eyes to stay open and adjust to the light of the sweltering desert afternoon rays. A glance above showed she was alone and a look down at her body showed she was wrapped up in a neon orange rock-climbing rope. Then she turned her head to the right and froze.

She had been placed on the edge of a cliff. One wrong move, and she would go over.

Was that the outcome expected of her? Would someone who found her body assume her death had been a climbing accident? She would be found all tied up as if her ropes did her in?

But why not just throw her over while she was unconscious?

Danika couldn't worry about that right now. She needed to put some space between her and this edge. Ever so carefully, she inched her way to the left, holding her breath until she knew there was a good foot between her and the ledge.

Moving her fingers, she attempted to grab at the rope near her wrists but to no avail. Wriggling her body didn't help to loosen the hold. She thought about calling out, but worried her abductor was close by. She still wondered why he hadn't killed her.

Danika rolled onto her side and then onto her belly, keeping her chin up to avoid having dirt in her face. She looked out across the vast desert, peering into the hazy burn of the sun. Visible heat waves shimmered off the hard ground. Sun-bleached stones riddled the terrain, surrounded by thorny shrubs. Something moved and caught her attention. She squinted to see a long, tan snake sunbathing on one of the rocks. Its coloring camouflaged with the stone beneath it.

Oh, please don't be venomous. She'd had her various run-ins with poisonous snakes. It came with the territory of rock climbing. But in the past, she had her legs and arms to put distance between them. She might as well be wrapped up with a bow as easy prey for this creature. She prayed it wouldn't notice her. If she just remained quiet, she might be able to shimmy herself farther from it.

"Danika!" Tru's voice broke through the heavy silence. More than anything she wanted to respond and tell him where she was. She feared any movement would alert the snake to her presence. But what if this was her only chance of being found and helped?

She knew snakes didn't hear as humans did, but rather through vibrations. A shout or a stomp on the ground would be heard and startle it. The slightest movement or sound vibration could cause it to strike.

"Danika!" he shouted again, but this time he sounded farther away as if he'd already run past her or was going in the wrong direction. If he went any farther, he might not come back this way. She could just as easily die on this ledge from sun exposure and heat.

Or a snake attack.

She had no choice but to respond. With her gaze locked on the snake, she said on a soft whisper, "Here!"

The snake didn't move.

She tried a bit louder. "I'm here!"

The snake lifted its head and flicked its tongue. Did it taste her fear?

A deep breath slowly escaped her lungs, and she called even louder. "Tru!" She cringed as she waited for the reptile's response.

It froze in place, now on high alert. Its intense black eyes stared right at her. She knew it could pull back and fling itself at her in a quick strike, and she would have no place to go and no way of fighting it off.

Heavy footsteps pounded the hard earth. "Danika!" Tru yelled, now so close.

"Shhh," she said, not that he could hear her. She needed some way to tell him to walk lightly before he came barreling into this area. A quick glance away from the snake, and she caught a flash of Tru's green T-shirt. Then she looked back at the snake. Her eyes flitted between the two of them until Tru slowed his steps in caution.

"Are you all right?" he whispered, his concern carrying to her on a whistling wind.

"Snake," she whispered.

He sighed. "Don't panic. It's going to be okay. We're in its territory. It will only attack if it feels provoked."

"I think it feels provoked. It's staring at me."

Tru laughed under his breath. "It has poor eyesight, so it probably isn't staring at you." He turned around and searched for something. Bending over for a few moments, he stood back up with a few rocks. Before she could stop him, he chucked them at the snake.

Danika inhaled in shock. Then she realized he hadn't thrown the rocks at the snake, but rather behind it. The creature whipped around and retreated into a crevice, slithering at a fast pace until it was gone.

Danika dropped her face forward, now able to finally breathe. But suddenly, she felt Tru at her side, untangling and loosening the ropes.

"Who did this?" he demanded.

"I don't know," she replied. "I was knocked out." She looked up to reference the bloody lump on her head. "When I heard a sound behind me, I started to turn but was grabbed. Then lights out. I woke up here, almost falling off the edge."

"They put you there." Tru held up the rope.

"Yeah, but why not just throw me over?" She sat up and swooned a bit. She touched her head and winced. "I mean this guy isn't afraid of killing people. He's proven that already."

"It was a warning. Or maybe it wasn't our killer. Perhaps someone assisting him, someone at the park." He sighed. "Maybe even a staff member."

Danika felt her eyes bulge. "Are you serious? Why would you say that?"

"Because my gear that was kept in my closet was tampered with. It had to be someone who would be familiar with where I kept my bag. Someone who would go unnoticed walking into my office. Someone who would know I'd be looking into this case and needing my gear."

"That doesn't sound like a safe work environment if someone wants to see you die in a tragic fall."

"No, it doesn't, and I mean to find the person and arrest them immediately. Can you stand?"

"I think so." She turned onto her knees and pushed up carefully.

"The more important question. Can you rappel down?"

"Absolutely." She reached for the rope. "At least the guy left us this." She touched her aching head. "Climbing back down would have been tough."

"And climbing up wasn't? You amaze me." He laughed under his breath as he scanned the area. "Let's see where we can tie this to and get down there." He moved to find the place they had ascended from. "I also think we need to rethink this partnership. It's not safe. This guy sabotaged my ropes and was willing to kill me. I don't doubt they'll come after you if they think you're investigating too."

Danika thought of the man in the visitor center store. He had been looking over her shoulder at all her maps and books. "I have a feeling it's too late for that. In fact, I would be willing to say when I return to my car, I will also have my gear tampered with."

Tru found a place to tie off the rope that gave them plenty of length to make the descent. "Then I would say you will not be going anywhere near the caves. It's not safe."

Danika grabbed hold of the rope and jumped down backward off the edge. "Sorry, Tru, but I'm going with or without you." And with that, she rappelled down, showing she had what it took to make it through the caves. She hit the ground and looked up at his stern face. "You coming or not?" she hollered up.

An exasperated sigh escaped his lips, but he took the rope and zipped down with ease. So well that she was almost content with him to take the lead.

Almost.

Tru decided to return to his makeshift office at the Lechuguilla Cave. Knowing that someone had been in his formal office at headquarters gave him concern about returning there for the private conversation he needed to have with Danika. Someone believed him to be a threat, and he didn't want to lead anyone to her. One of his team members was a traitor, and all that mattered was that he kept her safe.

"Where are we going?" she asked from beside him in his Jeep.

"Back to my tent. We'll have more privacy there. The fewer people that see us together the better for you. What I really should be doing is calling park patrol to handle my break-in. The shooting didn't happen on park property, so that's under the Bureau of Land Management's jurisdiction. But the tampering of my gear did, and they really should know about it. Part of me wants to call them, but the other part of me wants to figure out who on my team is untrustworthy first. No sense in alerting the guy that we're onto him." He glanced her way and saw the crusted blood on top of her head. "Are you sure you don't need a doctor?"

"I'm sure. It looks worse than it is. I've had my share of head wounds when I've slipped and taken a tumble. Whatever this guy hit me with is nothing compared to solid rock."

Tru took the next turn back into park property but bypassed headquarters for the road he needed to get to the cave. "Look, Danika, I understand you have experience with climbing. What you did back there was astonishing, but caving takes more than experienced climbing. The falls that can occur are done in pitch-black darkness at over one hundred feet drops. I've seen people fall on other people and kill them. We have caves that are for tourists. They've been approved and deemed safe. But what you're planning to do by going into these uncharted caves, deep into the earth, could lead you down a tunnel with no end, or worse, no outlet. You get stuck, you have about three days before you're dead."

"I understand." She took out her phone and pulled something up on the screen. "That's why before I go into anything I want to make sure I'm going into the right cave. These images and this map are where I need to be." She held up the phone to show an image of Slaughter Canyon. It was the canyon they apprehended the shooter in.

"So this is why you were in that area in the first place."

"Your ranger assistant told me where this picture was taken."

"*My* ranger assistant?" Concern and curiosity sparked his interest. At this point anyone on his team was suspect. "Which one?"

"Um… I can't member her name. She had red braids. Something that began with an *S*."

"Stacy?"

"Yes! Stacy. That's right. I showed her the picture after you refused to help me. She came running over to me while I was getting into my car. She had said you wouldn't help me but was willing to take a look. She knew right away it was Slaughter Canyon."

The paved road ended, and he drove his Jeep over rocky terrain. He pulled up to his tent and parked.

"Where is everyone?" Danika asked. "Last time I was here there were a lot of people hanging out."

"That's because we had a survey going on. The day you arrived I was coming out of a four-day trek inside the cave. Whenever we go in, we have to have a team of medical personnel, rescuers and such outside waiting just in case something goes wrong."

"In other words, a rescue team."

Tru studied her face as another concern for partnering with her came to light. "Or a recovery team. Not everyone comes out alive. Sometimes we can carry them back out and sometimes a team has to go in for them."

She frowned and dropped her gaze to her phone.

"There's something I have to ask you," he said.

She looked back at him warily and with the downward tilt to her head. Her long hair that had come loose

from her ponytail fell to her shoulder. "Okay?" The
concern on her face said it wasn't.

Too bad.

"When you found the dead body, you froze." He
waited for her to deny it.

Instead, remorse and disappointment showed on her
face. She gave a short, single nod. "It won't happen
again."

"How can you be so sure? What happened down
there to cause you to react that way? I couldn't even
get you to answer a simple question. If I take you down
into these caves—"

"I said it wouldn't happen again." Intense annoyance filled her eyes, but he was glad to see her bravado
was back. Perhaps she was strong enough to make
the journey into the underworld. "I know why it happened, and I won't let it get to me again. Can we just
leave it at that?" She opened the passenger door and
got out. Before she closed the door, she turned back
to him and said, "Please."

Her words told him there was more than finding a
dead guy that caused her to react in such a way.

Something personal.

"Have you seen a dead body before, Danika?" he
asked. "Perhaps someone you knew?"

She dropped her gaze and pressed her lips tight. Her
eyes drifted closed on a sigh. "My dad. I found him
with a gunshot to his head. They deemed it suicide."
She lifted her gaze and looked him straight in the eyes.
This time anger reflected back at him. Her blue gaze
turned stormy and driven. "I disagree." With that she
slammed the door and walked to the tent.

EIGHT

Danika stepped foot inside Tru's makeshift office. It was a white canvas tent with nothing but the table she had stood over the last time she was here, a small chest in the corner and a foldable desk for him in the back center. The middle of the tent had a wooden beam that held up the roofline. As she waited for him to follow her in, she paced back and forth in an attempt to regain her composure. She hadn't wanted to talk about her father, especially to Tru. She wasn't ready to trust him with this personal information.

"I'm sorry for pushing," he spoke from the opened tent flaps. "I suspected it was personal, and I should have left it at that. If it helps, I know how you feel. And maybe that's why I can be so demanding about the safety of cavers. I've seen the result when people aren't cautious."

Was he talking about Melinda? Now Danika wanted to push him for more information. He owed her, she thought. "Can you tell me what happened to her? The only message we received was Melinda was killed in a caving accident. No details of how it happened, only that she fell. She was the best climber. She was the best lead."

"You were her second?" His eyes widened as his face blanched. "I knew you knew her but…"

"She made me a better climber…a better person. Her faith…" Danika couldn't explain what it was Melinda had. But she knew she wanted it.

"I know." Tru whispered. He came around the other side of his desk and pulled up two camp chairs. Placing them beside each other, he waved his hand to offer her one. "Please sit. I can't have this conversation standing."

After a moment of hesitation, she reluctantly took the chair, but moved it a foot farther away from his. "So, yes, I knew her very well. We met at university in my freshman year. I had always been a climber. It was just something I did with my father. But I lacked technique. Melinda had already been competing for years. She was breaking records left and right. But one day, out of the whole group, she pointed to me and said, 'Hey you, let's go. Let's see what you've got as my second.' I looked over my shoulder thinking she was talking to someone else." Danika faced him and couldn't hold back her disdain for him this moment. "You took her from me. And I don't mean because of her death."

He tilted his head with a confused look on his face. "How?"

"Because she took one look at you and fell in love. You became more important than climbing…than me. And all of a sudden, I was without my partner."

Tru began to open his mouth but quickly shut it and

nodded. "I'm sorry. I know that doesn't help, but that semester was a whirlwind. I knew the moment that I met her that I was going to marry her." He dropped his head, looking at his folded hands in his lap. "Or at least I thought I would." He glanced over at her. "I never gave the other people in her life a thought. Beyond meeting her family, anyway. I know you don't care, but she filled a role that I very much needed at the time. My own family had fragmented, and we dispersed all over the state. We're still pretty much separated. When Melinda came into my life, I thought I would have a family again." He shrugged. "I was wrong. About everything. I am sorry. So very sorry."

Suddenly, Danika didn't think he was talking about his remorse for taking her climbing partner away from her. This apology was for something else.

"Do you blame yourself for her death?" she asked.

"It was my job to keep her safe. I shouldn't have brought her so far down into the cavern. It was too soon."

Danika sputtered a laugh. "You know we're talking about Melinda, right? There wasn't a boulder she said no to. She lived with no fear. Her faith never let her. But she also always knew the risks."

Tru whistled a slow release of air as though he was mentally preparing to say something. "Okay. I took her down into Lechuguilla." He glanced in the direction of the cave outside the tent. "We were on a survey. I wanted to show her this untouched pool of water the color of a Caribbean teal blue. It's stunning and matched the color of her…" He looked at her and cleared his throat. "Well, you know."

Danika nodded, remembering her friend's pretty eyes. "They were always so bright and filled with joy."

He smiled and laughed a bit. "For sure," he whispered. "Anyway…" He cleared his throat again. "I let her take the lead." He squeezed his eyes tight. "It was wrong. I was wrong."

The picture of what happened to her friend became clear in an instant. "No. You were in love," Danika simply said. "Saying no to her was impossible. Just like the day she pointed at me and said, 'Let's go.' There was no way to say no to her."

"Especially with those eyes." He smiled, then frowned. "They were the last thing I saw of her in my headlight. She held on to the rope to rappel down a 185-foot drop. I leaned down to kiss her, but she smiled and kicked off, saying, 'Too slow.'" His throat convulsed, and he jumped up so fast his camp chair flipped back onto the canvas floor. "We should get back to work… I need to figure out who is this traitor on my team. That's all that matters right now."

"She fell," Danika said in a low voice. It really was a simple accident. "Melinda made a wrong move, and she fell."

"I should've gone first. It was my survey, and I broke the rules. I really don't want to talk about this anymore." He walked over to the table with the working map of the cave. He put both his hands on the edge and leaned over, but she could tell he wasn't even looking at it. He was taking a moment to regroup.

"It wasn't your fault," she said reluctantly. "I'll be honest. I really wanted it to be. For three years, I took solace thinking that it was. I needed to place blame, but that stops today." Danika stood up and walked over to stand beside him at the table. She studied the map, and without a second thought said, "Where did she die?"

His gaze went to a certain place on the map, and she followed it. When he didn't reach to point to the place, she did. He nodded his response. "Every time I pass by the spot, I have to stop and take a few moments."

Danika couldn't tell the exact distance the location was from the opening of the cave, but she didn't think it was that far in. "I know this cavern is gigantic, but is it possible for you to take me there...right now?"

His head turned quickly at her. "It's too dangerous."

"Not any more dangerous than any other cave I'll be going into. Consider it training. Please." She covered his hand closest to her with her own. It was just a gentle touch, but she realized it was their first. And in this moment, it felt personal, as though he was her connection to her friend.

He looked down at where she held on to him. She could see his hesitancy, and with the repeated shake of his head, the answer was bound to be no. She hadn't earned his trust yet. But then, she hadn't been completely honest with him either. She withheld the information about her father's death, and how she believed it was someone in this smuggling operation that killed him. She withheld the fact that these artifacts were discovered by him, and she wanted them back. She wondered why she hesitated in sharing this information and knew that it had something to do with not knowing if Tru would return these artifacts to their rightful people, or if they would just end up behind a glass display in his visitor center.

With his other hand he reached over and covered hers. "You are so strong." He lifted her hand up and studied it. He held it so gently in his palm that tears pricked her eyes. "Watching you climb that boulder defied gravity. And I know you think Melinda was the best climber, but I never saw her do what you did today. She was brave, but sometimes she could be reckless." Tru lifted his gaze to hers. "Danika, I need to know that you won't be reckless. That you will listen to my every word and follow my every direction. Not just in this cave but all of them. Can you do that?"

Danika could see the two of them were at a pivotal moment in this relationship of sorts. He needed to know if he could trust her, just as much as she needed to know if she could trust him.

His green eyes glittered with intensity and pain. No matter what she said to him today about Melinda's death not being his fault, he still blamed himself.

Her heart softened. She thought maybe it was out of pity—because it couldn't be anything more than that. Regardless of the reason, she felt better working with him knowing the truth of Melinda's death now. Typically, she was no one's second, but in this situation, and under the circumstances, she could resign herself to the new role.

Danika turned her hand over in his palm and gripped it for a firm handshake. "Tru Butler, we have a killer to find. Because of that, I'll concede. You can take the lead, and I will follow your every command."

The mouth of the Lechuguilla Cave sat high up on a plateau to the north of the gypsum planes that extended to Texas. Beneath the limestone ground was a world made up of passages and desolate rock rooms.

"The cave was found fifty years ago. Before that, no one knew it existed," Tru explained from beside Danika. They each wore side packs with their gear. They tested these to make sure they hadn't been tampered with, although the rigging in the cave had been left from the last survey. They had some just in case. It still didn't make Tru feel any better about bringing her in.

"There's not much out here. The land is so barren. Just desert as far as the eye can see."

Tru pointed. "It's over there." The ground sloped downward and then up again. The first splash of green came into view. "See the cacti? That's where we're heading."

"It doesn't look like much," Danika said. "I don't even see an opening." She shivered and looked to the sky. The sun was setting on the day, taking its heat with it. "Will we be walking through the night?"

"The next time you see the sun it will be coming up from the east." He looked in the opposite direction from where the sun was setting. "I have to be honest— I don't feel good about this."

She stopped and grabbed his forearm. "I know what I'm doing. And it seems fitting to start here. It's almost like I'm receiving Melinda's blessing."

Tru glanced in the direction of the black hole. Once they went down anything could happen.

"Tru, we went through the map. You've given me thorough directions, and we are as prepared as we can be."

Tru led the rest of the way to where some oak trees

had taken root by the entrance. Within some rocks a twenty-foot-wide, thirty-foot-long entrance awaited. He began checking ropes that were still secured by bolts to a nearby tree. He threaded the rope through his rappel rack and made sure she knew to do the same when it was her turn. They put their gloves on, and he stepped back into darkness, saying, "On rope." He rappelled down into the black hole, and when he hit the ground, he called up, "Off rope."

A few moments later, Danika called out the same commands and soon stood beside him in the tight quarters of the cave. He flicked on his headlamp to look into her face.

No fear.

There was no sense in asking her if she wanted to turn back.

"So that was a hundred-foot drop?" she asked.

"That was sixty." He turned to lead the way through the colorless and dirty shaft. "Careful, the floor is uneven. And there are a lot of piles of dirt from recent digs. This area was originally called Old Misery Pit."

"Seems appropriate," she mumbled. He didn't respond as he came to the next drop. He picked up a nylon rope waiting there and wove it through the metal ladder of his rack. "This is only ten feet, but it smells pretty bad down there. On rope." He descended and waited for her to join him.

The area was even smaller than the first. Just a small rectangle that barely fit them. When she stood in front of him, he could feel the warmth of her breath and how her breathing had picked up.

"Are you okay?" he asked.

She put her hand on his chest and nodded. She offered him a slight smile. "This is fun." The nervousness in her eyes told him she was trying to make light of her trepidation. He was glad to see she was afraid.

Melinda hadn't been.

"We have to crawl now." He reached for her gloved hand on his chest and brought her down to the floor. He led the way to a manhole cover on a hinge and readied to swing it wide. "Cover your eyes. It's going to blow dust into them when I open this. This was installed to stabilize the entrance and protect the cave. It'll be a twenty-foot drop."

When she turned away, he used his weight to swing the heavy cover open and expose the drainpipe that descended down. The pressure released air past them on a whoosh. Once it stabilized, he looked at her and said, "It's not too late."

She hesitated but after a few deep breaths she said, "Lead me."

Tru huffed a short laugh. He found this woman to be intriguing. The fact that she was a private investigator made her even more so. "In your investigations, have you ever put yourself down into a drain to solve a case?"

She smiled and visibly relaxed. "There's a first time for everything."

"Ladies first. I have to close it behind me."

Danika threaded her rope through her rack. "On rope," she said, but before she could disappear into the darkness, panic filled his chest.

"Wait." He reached for her ropes. "I just need to check. Humor me."

She shook her head as he checked her ropes. "It's no joke. Check all you want."

Her understanding of how hard this was for him endeared her to him in an instant. But it also made him worry even more about bringing her into danger. "You're a good person, Danika Lewis. Thank you."

In the brightness of his headlight, he watched her frown and look away. Before he could say anything, she descended the pipe. Her suspicious expression raised a flag.

Danika Lewis may be a good person, but she was definitely hiding something. And if he was going to lead her to the center of the earth, there could be no secrets between them.

NINE

"Off rope," Danika yelled up the pipe for Tru to begin his descent. The culvert dropped her into a crawl space just like the one she had just left. To make room for Tru she crawled a few feet away. When she felt him behind her, she moved aside for him to pass by.

"It's going to get very tight for a little while, then it will open up. I promise. Just stay close behind." He led the way, and she followed as close to his boots as possible.

She never thought of herself as claustrophobic, but she couldn't deny that her lungs felt like they were compressing. "Tru, I can't breathe," she gasped.

"I know. There's not much air in here. It's just a little farther. Stay with me." He moved on, and she did her best to take short breaths with each movement.

Finally, the passage opened, and Danika sat up a little higher to gasp for more air. "Where are we now?" She tried to remember the map she had studied in the tent. But that miniature drawing did not compare to reality.

Tru shone a light to her right and revealed a gigantic

tunnel of smooth walls and formations. Delicate towers rose up from the floor at least six feet high while the ceiling dripped liquid stone. She gasped again, but this time it wasn't for air.

"I've never seen anything so stunning. And to think no one has ever seen this… I mean, besides you and the survey teams."

He huffed and stood up. "This is nothing. We're not even in the cave yet." He offered her a hand and helped her onto her feet. "You breathing better?"

"I think so."

He shone his light into her face, blinding her. "You have to know. There can be no uncertainty down here. If you're not ready to go on, then we don't. One wrong move, one wrong slip, and it's over. Do you understand?"

She swallowed so hard her gulp practically echoed in the chamber. "I'm ready."

"Stay right behind me. The floor drops unexpectedly. I've been down here enough times to know whereabouts. I won't lead you over." With that he headed down the long corridor with her on his heels.

Just as he said, within a couple hundred yards, the floor disappeared into a deep, dark pit. Water dripped around her and echoed up from below. With the beam of his light, she watched him grab the climbing rope anchored to one of the stalagmites.

"This place is called Boulder Falls," he told her.

"A problem," she responded.

"At 185 feet, yes, it's a big problem."

Danika chewed on her lower lip as she considered the problem before her. She wasn't afraid of rappelling, but she didn't realize how deep into the earth this trek would take her. "Are all caves this deep?"

Tru paused and set her rope up into her rack. "We don't have to go on. And no, not all of them are this deep. That's why finding this was a major discovery. And we still haven't found the other end. We may never find it. At least not in my lifetime."

Danika frowned in the dark. "I think I understand what drove Melinda in coming down here. She wanted to solve the problem. As a climber, that is our goal. And we don't stop until we do. How much farther did she get?"

Tru didn't answer.

Danika could hear his breathing pick up, and she reached out to find his hand. Their gloves kept her from making contact fully, but she held on as best she could to get his attention.

"Tell me," she whispered.

"She didn't."

Danika dropped her hand and looked down into the black void of Boulder Falls. This was where her friend died.

Particularly, at the bottom.

"I think we should just go back," Tru said. "I don't want anything bad to happen to you. I brought you to the place where I last saw her alive. Can that just be enough?" He began unfastening the rope from her ladder rack.

She reached out and attempted to stop his rapid movements. "I can do this."

Tru studied her face. Would he put an end to this

endeavor? After a few moments, he retightened the rope to her rack and double-checked for safety.

Without further delay, she slid down to prepare for the descent. "On rope," she said and looked up at him. He knelt down and brought his face within inches of hers. For a moment she thought he was going to kiss her. But why would he do such a thing? The idea brought a little panic into her.

But also, a little curiosity.

The thought stunned her and she felt guilty, knowing this was the man Melinda had been in love with. He was the man she was going to spend the rest of her life with, and the man she walked away from friendships for.

"Don't kiss me," she said quickly.

He flinched and pulled back. Then he laughed. "I wasn't planning to. I was just going to say that I would be right behind you, unless you wanted some time alone down there."

"Oh." Now she felt silly. But instead of making things even more awkward, she laughed with him. "That's a kind gesture, thank you. But if it's all right with you, I really don't want to be down there alone."

He gave a firm nod. "Then I'll join you right away. Go ahead. I'll see down there."

She dropped back and began the descent. One hundred eighty-five feet felt like forever. With each passing foot, she wondered about Melinda taking this fall. Danika looked up and watched as Tru's headlamp grew dimmer and dimmer as she put more distance between them, until it faded away completely.

Her shallow breathing returned but not from lack of air. This was total fear.

The moment her feet touched, she cried out, "Off rope!" She heard tears in her voice and realized she was crying. At least her blurred vision wouldn't matter down here in the pitch black.

"On rope!" Tru's voice sounded so far away. The distance between them became even greater with that realization. The wait only made it worse.

Danika peered around her with her single lamp. The space wasn't much bigger than a table. She didn't even think there was space to lay down. She wept for her friend, who lost her life in such a small, dark place. She fell to her knees and whispered, "I forgive you."

Danika didn't know where those words came from, but she knew she had to say them so she could move on from the loss she still felt at the absence of her friend. The absence that started long before Melinda died.

The day Tru Butler entered Melinda's life.

The thought of the man brought Danika's attention back to the fact that he had not arrived yet. She peered up into the dark tunnel above but saw no sign of him.

"Tru? Is everything all right?" she called up. Remembering how he'd told her people had died when cavers fell on another, she stepped away from the rope until her back hit the smooth wall. "Tru?" she called again, hearing her rapid heartbeat in her head. "I said you didn't have to wait!" She heard the whining in her voice.

Or was that panic and terror?

Danika learned something about herself in that moment. She was afraid of the dark.

"Tru!"

Tru felt the anchor begin to give way when he was about halfway down Boulder Falls. He couldn't explain it, but he felt a shift in the rope. The movement caused him to lock his legs on the wall and freeze. From below, he could hear Danika call up to him, but he didn't dare reply. Not until he knew he was secure and wouldn't cause a complete tear away.

Without letting go of the rope, he reached the other hand to the wall for something to hold on to.

The wall was smooth as glass.

He had a choice to make. Attempt to climb back up and check the anchor or continue down slowly and hope he was wrong about it.

"Tru!" Danika called again, fear threading through her voice now. The painful sound caused a shiver to race up his spine. If something happened to her, he would never forgive himself. He was the lead, and he led her to the bottom of a pit…just as he had Melinda.

He wouldn't leave Danika behind.

With his decision made, Tru continued down the rope in a slow, cautious manner. He did his best to stay close to the wall as much as possible and keep his feet searching for places to lock into. Having been up and down this rope many times, he typically had a good estimate of where he was and how much farther he had to go. But at this slow pace, he could only guess.

The rope caught again.

Tru froze and could hear his erratic breathing. He forced himself to blow out his anxiety and breathe deep to stay calm. It couldn't be much longer.

He hoped.

And then what? Why hadn't he thought of what came next? He couldn't put Danika back on this rope. One slip could have been his imagination. But two? At 185 feet he wouldn't risk it.

He had to climb back up. He had no other choice but to leave her behind.

No, not leave her behind. He would return for her. He would make sure the rope was safe, secure and anchored correctly. He had no doubt she would be able to climb back up, and if she couldn't, he would get her harness and lift her out…also just as he had Melinda.

With his mind made up, he called down to Danika, "I have to return to the top. Something is wrong with the anchor. I'll come back for you. I promise."

"Please don't leave me down here!" Her terror pricked his eyes with tears. He squeezed them closed to fight against dropping down the rest of the way.

"I promise I will be back. I just don't think the anchor is secure. If both of us are stuck down there—" The rope slipped again, and he gave a shout, "Get out of the way!"

A grinding sound echoed through the chamber and shook the rope in his hands. Dust drifted down onto his face. Whatever was happening above went beyond the anchor. The formation that the anchor was attached to was shifting.

Or separating from the cave.

The idea was unfathomable, but Tru had no time to evaluate the cause. Not while he hung from a rope with an unknown amount of space between him and the floor.

"Cover your head!" he shouted down as more dust fell from the ceiling and forced his eyes closed. He inhaled it through his mouth and nostrils and choked. The whole cave could come down on them.

"I am! What's happening?" Danika's panicked muffled voice rose to him. He couldn't tell her. The terror growing in him silenced him. He felt useless, hanging between life and death.

An eerie silence filled the cavern, and for a moment he hoped all would be well. Then a smattering of small rocks touched his ear and cheek as they fell from above. They stung his skin as they went by. He coughed to clear his throat in the relative quiet as stillness reigned. The sounds echoed off the rocks.

The calm before the storm?

He prayed not.

"Dear God, You tell us not to fear, and I am making that commitment right now. Whatever happens, I trust You." He spoke the words aloud into the silent cavern. His trembling voice negated his words, but he spoke from the heart.

Craning his neck back, he peered straight up with the light from his headlamp. His rope was taut with the weight of his body. His legs were locked against the wall to keep him in place. If he could grab hold of something to take the weight off the rope, perhaps it would give Danika time to climb. She would need her climbing equipment to give her leverage along the way.

"Danika, you may need to climb up. Can you do that?"

"Y-yes. I think. It's hard to tell with the darkness. What are you planning?"

Tru felt the wall with one hand, seeking for something that would give him leverage. His hands felt a hole, and he sank his fingers into it. "I'm going to try to take my weight off the rope. I'll hold as long as I can while you climb."

"But what about you? I won't know how to fix this. And what if it comes down?"

"I have to have faith that you will figure it out or get help. I've seen you climb. I know you can do this." He could hear her breathing heavily, and that told him he might not be that far from the bottom. Maybe letting go of the rope and jumping would be better.

The grinding sound returned, canceling his thoughts. His rope dropped at least half a foot and caught again. It rested, but before he could take another breath a large crack echoed through the chamber, and he hurtled to the floor below.

"Out of the way!" He tried to yell but wasn't sure he even got the words out. His neck whipped back with the suddenness of his descent. His stomach was left above, and his lungs emptied out in a whoosh. He landed hard on his back but knew what was coming next.

At 185 feet above, a large boulder with an anchor and rope attached was about to come crashing down. Where it landed was anyone's guess.

With the wind knocked out of him, he couldn't verbalize this fact. "Get…to…the wall," he managed to breathe out.

Suddenly, he could feel Danika's hands on him. He tried to push her away, but his hands wouldn't work. In one swoop, she rolled him over until he hit the wall.

In the next second, the rock hit the floor right where he had been lying. The crash shook his whole body and rang through his ears. The echo continued to reverberate up and down the chamber.

And he had no idea where Danika was. Had the boulder landed on her instead?

TEN

Danika hit the wall with her back just as the large boulder came barreling down and smashed against the floor. The air rushed from her lungs as she slid to the floor and landed with a thud. She could only hope she had pushed Tru out of the way in time before flinging herself back against the wall.

Through the light of her headlamp, she could make out the shape of one of the formations she had seen above. Now sitting on the floor in front of her, it looked so much larger than it had when she walked past it. It didn't seem possible that something so large and formidable could just come undone.

And now it sat between her and Tru.

"Please tell me you're all right," she said. She held her breath waiting for a response, hoping she would get one.

"I'm alive," he said quietly.

Not the answer she was hoping for. "I asked if you were all right."

He didn't answer. That only told her he was trying to protect her from knowing the truth.

"How bad is it?" she asked.

"I can't move my leg. I can't tell if it's because I'm injured or because I'm pinned under the rock. Either way, I'm not getting out of here. Danika, you have to go up without me, but…" He took a deep breath and let it out slowly. She could hear the nervousness in him.

"What aren't you telling me?" She closed her eyes as she waited for the response.

"I don't think this was an accident. Which means someone else is in this cave with us. I could be sending you up there only to come face-to-face with whoever just tried to kill us. If I could go instead, I would."

"What makes you think someone did this?" Danika stood up and found her balance. She maneuvered her way around the large rock until Tru's headlamp could be seen. His face was shielded beneath the hat. She looked up into the black tunnel above.

"We anchored to this rock because it was secure. And I'm sure I heard a grinding sound before I felt the rope give way. Someone cut the rock. The added weight of my body just brought it down."

She scanned the length of his body as far as she could. Giving the rock a shove only proved it to be fruitless. The boulder wasn't going anywhere. "Do you have any pain?"

"Just a pressure," he replied. "It feels like someone is grabbing my ankle and I can't kick them off." She saw the shadow of his hands moving. Then he held something out in front of her. "Take this. Just in case."

She reached out and took something hard from him. "Is this what I think it is?" Her light shone down on what was in her hand.

A gun.

Stunned at first, all she could say was "I didn't even know rangers carried guns."

"Not all. Patrol definitely. But because I'm in charge of monitoring the caves, I'm able to make arrests... when I'm walking, that is." He sighed and put his head back against the wall. His light shone up above. "I just don't see any other way. You have to do this, or..."

She understood what he wasn't saying. Or they would both die down here.

"I'll go."

"When you make it out, I want you to call Bard. Don't go back to headquarters. Tell him where I am and to put a team together. Tell him my team is compromised. He's an investigator, but he's also my friend. I trust him. He'll know what to do. Then I want you to go back to your home. It's too dangerous for you now."

"No. I'm not going anywhere. The wedding is in three weeks. I still have to solve this case."

Tru groaned and it sounded as if he was trying to pull his leg free. He yelled out in anger. "It's no use." He huffed. "And I can't believe you're still talking about this wedding. Someone is trying to kill us. You need to get out of here."

"The fact that someone *is* trying to kill us tells me I am close. I'll climb up and call Bard, but I'm not going back to Texas without answers."

"Who hired you?" His question hung between them in silence. "Who are you investigating for?"

Danika stepped back into the darkness and away from his headlamp's beam. She didn't want to tell him this quest was her own. "That's confidential," she said.

"Well, I'm not guiding you into any more caves until I know."

The boulder between them was the biggest problem she had ever faced—and it wasn't the fallen rock. It was a lack of trust.

"Then I'll find a new guide as soon as I get out of here." She skirted the rock and reached for the wall. Feeling its smoothness, she opted for her temporary anchors from her side pack. In short, angry movements, she prepared her ropes and pullies, and started to feel the wall to know the best places to anchor them. Once ready to climb, she said, "Goodbye, Tru. I'll give your gun to Bard." And with that she began the ascension to the top. She wanted to say that she hoped his foot wasn't broken but pressed her lips closed. That felt too personal, as if they were friends.

And they weren't.

"Please be careful." Tru's voice drifted up to her, so low she almost missed it. "I'm sorry I let you down."

Danika's hand paused on the anchor she was in the process of fitting into a crevice. She thought about responding, but what could she say that would matter? Their paths crossed, and now their lives would go on as if it never happened. She sighed and said, "You didn't let me down. I'm grateful you brought me to this place. If nothing else, it means a lot to me to see where Melinda died. You've given me closure, so… thank you." She didn't wait for any response but continued up the wall.

Before she arrived at Carlsbad Caverns, she probably would've thought it was fitting to leave Tru Butler in the exact spot where Melinda had died. She had believed he was to blame and should spend the rest of his life being reminded of that. But now, having seen the place and knowing the details, she knew Melinda would not want her blaming this man for something that was out of his control. With each foot that Danika put behind her of this 185-foot climb, she knew that one slipup would be the end of her.

And Melinda had known it too.

Danika could feel the perspiration running down from her temples and the center of her back as she strained to lift herself up foot by foot. The rope she used would give her a ten-foot fall if she slipped, but that was only if her anchors held. As she secured each one, she did her best to test them before putting her full weight on them. Without Melinda as her lead, Danika had become accustomed to being both the lead and the second. Never had she thought that she was being prepared for such a time as this.

Danika had a while to ponder things as she ascended the wall, and when she reached the top, she pushed herself up and over the top of the wall. She gave herself a moment to let her muscles relax. She still had more to climb before she could radio Bard for help, and after taking a few breaths, she pushed herself up to stand. The stunning corridor loomed in front of her with all its formations of stalagmites and stalactites. Many of the columns nearly touched each other where they had dripped and formed over the years. Some were skinny, some were thick. As she passed by one of the wider ones, a light turned on and stopped her cold.

In the next second, someone stepped out from behind the column and shone their headlamp into her face, blinding her.

"Give me the gun," he said in a low, gruff voice. "And don't say a word." He lifted his own right at her and gave her no choice but to comply.

Long past the time he watched Danika disappear into the dark, Tru turned his headlamp off to conserve the battery and continued to pull and push and twist his foot in the hopes it would release. His whole leg ached, which he took as a good sign. If he could feel pain, then perhaps nothing was damaged, and he was just pinned.

The thought of breaking his foot in an attempt to maneuver it out of its wedged position crossed his mind. But then he still had to climb Boulder Falls and walk out of here. If Danika left him down here to rot, he might have no other choice but to try. Until then he would wait. He thought by now she should at least be to the manhole. Soon she would have a signal and be able to call Bard.

If the bad guy hadn't taken her out.

Tru pulled his leg as hard as he could, hating this feeling of uselessness. He needed to get out of here. He needed to make sure she made it out alive. In the next second, he heard something clatter beside him. The abrupt sound jolted him, and he sat up straight. Turning his light back on, he searched the area that he could see. Shadows and contorted images of rocks and crevices made it difficult to figure out what had come crashing down.

Then he saw it.

His own gun.

Tru looked up into the dark void. "Danika!" Had she dropped it? If someone was up there somewhere, she would need it for protection. He'd made sure it was secured to her before she started the climb. He checked the cartridge.

Empty.

Which could only mean one thing.

She hadn't dropped it. Instead, it was taken off her, emptied and thrown back to him to show she had been overtaken.

Tru resumed his efforts to break free, using all his might to budge the boulder even a fraction of an inch. Sweat poured down his face as he attempted to move the rock.

Truth settled around him as softly as the dust falling from above earlier.

The killer had Danika.

ELEVEN

Danika's helmet was gone. The first thing the man who came out of the shadows did was remove her light…after he took Tru's gun. With his own head-lamp, his face disappeared into darkness, blinding her to even look at him.

"Who are you?" she asked as he held his own gun in the center of her back. She didn't expect a response. The only other word he'd said to her after he demanded the gun was "Move." Since that moment, his gun had been pointed in the center of her back as he forced her to lead the way out of the cave.

She believed they were about to approach the man-hole cover. She would have to climb the rope anchored there. She wondered who would go up first. If he went, she could try to crawl and hide somewhere in the cave, but he could just shut the manhole cover and leave them down here. The fact that he was leading her out told her he didn't want her dead.

"If you meant for us to die you would have just locked us down here." She hoped her reasoning didn't give him ideas.

He pushed his gun harder into her back as his answer. He managed to put it between two ribs, causing her to whimper in pain. He may want her alive, but that didn't mean she would come out unscathed.

With only a glimmer of his headlamp shining the path in front of her, Danika had to feel her way along the tight confines of the cave. She'd tripped twice, so now he held on to her shoulder with his free hand. His grip was tight and painful.

The shadow of the rope and the manhole pipe came into view. She stopped at the base and waited for his direction. If he let her go first, she thought she would be able to race to the top and run ahead to the exit. But if he went first, she could refuse to climb and call his bluff.

His delay in giving her directions told her he was considering the same outcomes.

"Well?" she said. "What's it going to be?"

Suddenly, she felt his hot breath on her neck. She cringed as a shiver ran down her spine. "That depends on how much you want to know the truth." He spoke in a whisper and remained close as she made the decision.

Truth about what? Her mind raced at what this meant. The truth about her father? The truth about the missing artifacts? The truth about the formation breaking and sending Tru down Boulder Falls? The truth about Dr. Elliot and his role in all this?

Before she could say a word and make her decision, the man pushed at her shoulder and brought her down to the floor. With her face to the ground, she felt his gun lift from her back and heard him quickly climb the rope. By the time she lifted her face and got to her knees, he was on the other side of the manhole cover looking down at her with his blinding light.

"Well?" he said. "What's it going to be?" He threw the same words she had said back at her. She had thought she would be calling his bluff, but instead he was calling hers.

Did she have any other choice but to go wherever it was he was leading her?

Danika closed her eyes and took a deep breath. Wherever he was taking her, there might be an opportunity to break away and get help for Tru. If he shut that manhole cover, there would be no opportunity at all. She and Tru would die down here in the dark underworld in a matter of days, if that.

Danika put one hand on the rope, then the other. With her mind made up, she hiked herself up onto the rope with her feet on the wall and climbed up and through the hole. As soon as she passed through, the man grabbed her under the arm and threw her back in front of him.

In the next second, he slammed the manhole cover down with a loud bang, sending a final message to Tru. If he could hear it, what would he think? Would he wonder if she closed it on him? That she was never coming back?

She didn't know if she was either.

The gun jammed into her ribs again, pushing her forward. All she knew was that she was walking toward the truth. Whether that was the truth she was looking for, or the truth of what would happen to her, she had no idea.

They had another rope to go up, and when they

reached it, the same protocol took place. He pushed her to the floor on her face while he stepped past her to ascend first. But as soon as she surfaced at the top, he covered her head with a plastic bag. She should have expected to be blindfolded, but this was more than being blindfolded. He cinched it closed around her neck, cutting off her air.

"I'd say you got about five minutes of oxygen." He grabbed her shoulder again and pushed her forward until they came to the last climb. This time he let her go first, by putting her hands on the rope and shoving her up.

Danika climbed as fast as she could, and as soon as she fell out of the hole onto the sand, she pulled at the bag to try to take it off her head. When it didn't budge, she pulled at the plastic and tried to tear it, but by then he had surfaced and grabbed her hands and tied them behind her back. He pushed her forward to keep walking.

Her air became thin. She did her best to take short, small breaths, so as not to use up all the oxygen she had left. Her lungs ached, and she felt herself sweating. The sun had gone down, and the desert heat had abated, but her body still reacted to her imminent suffocation.

She thought she would have to walk a far distance and feared she wouldn't make it. But before she made it ten steps, the man swept up her legs and picked her up, placing her down on something hard.

"Don't move, or I'll cut you," he whispered, and then suddenly she felt a blade next to her lips.

She froze in fear, attempting to swallow hard a

scream bubbling up in her throat. She sucked in the last remaining bits of air. Then air whooshed into her lungs all at once.

The bang of a car door slamming jolted her as she realized he'd cut a hole into the bag to give her air. The start of a motor and movement beneath her told her he was taking her somewhere and she was in the trunk.

But she was still alive.

With everything Danika had in her, she began to kick and scream. Would someone hear her outside?

But where?

She was in the middle of the desert with nothing but tumbleweeds and snakes. It was also in the middle of the night.

No one would be around.

She thought of her cell phone in her side pack and Tru's ranger radio he had slipped in. With her hands bound, she didn't think she could get to them no matter how much she strained.

But that wouldn't stop her from trying.

Danika pulled her arms apart so hard to try to break the bindings. Tears pricked her eyes from the pain at her wrists as well as the feeling of hopelessness. She jostled around as the vehicle sped up over uneven ground, jarring her teeth from the impacts of rocks and holes. Just when she thought this harsh trip would not end, the vehicle came to a screeching halt.

The driver's door was opened and slammed shut. The trunk was opened quickly after, and she was lifted out again and tossed onto the ground, unceremoniously.

She cried out in pain at not being able to catch the

fall and landing on her side and head. "Where am I?" she called out, panic lacing her voice.

The crunch of footsteps on rocky gravel retreated, and she heard the driver's door open again. But before it slammed shut, the man said, "This is the cave you're looking for." The next moment, the door closed, and the car revved its engine, pelting gravel and sand her way as it took off.

Danika quieted her racing heart, and for a few moments let his words sink in. Her fingers, still tied behind her back, grappled at the ground. She was outside in sand and rocks and probably miles from another human being. But his mention of the cave that she was looking for could only mean one thing.

He had brought her to the place she had been seeking…only to leave her here alone and still bound and blindfolded. To be so close to the place she had worked so hard to find for eight years, but not be able to see it felt more torturous than the gun to her back had been.

Danika pushed herself up to sit, feeling with her feet to get her bearings. She didn't dare get up and start walking around. The mouth of the cave could be nothing more than a hole in the ground and could be another 185-foot death drop.

Or more.

The idea was enough to paralyze her, but after the night sounds of the desert, filled with creepy crawlies and howling winds, she knew she couldn't remain there waiting to be bitten by a scorpion. She turned her body to feel more of her surroundings with her feet. With the sweep of her right boot, she kicked something small, sending it somewhere to her right.

Carefully using her legs to drag herself inch by inch, she made contact again with the object. Twisting around to use her fingers, she captured it and realized in an instant what she held.

The man left her the knife.

Danika went to work quickly and efficiently to cut through the bindings until her left hand loosened from the hold. As soon as she could move it, she pulled it through and clawed at the bag, tearing it from her face and eyes.

Darkness loomed and gave her no indication of her location. But the dark entrance to a cave stood off to the side behind some shadowy shrubs. It beckoned to her with its deep passage of long held secrets. She realized she still had her side pack with its climbing supplies. Though she had no headlamp.

Or a guide.

No, her guide was pinned under a boulder in another cave and needed her help to get him out. She wanted to tell him the cave might have been found. Nothing was definite, as this man might be sending her down the wrong path.

But why not just kill her if he meant her harm? Why not just leave her out here to die from the elements? Which could still happen if she didn't find help.

For both her and Tru.

Danika opened her side pack and removed her cell phone. She quickly realized she had no service out here. Frustration set in as she held it up to the night sky to no avail.

Then she dug around her pack and found the radio that Tru had put in there.

She smiled. Her guide had thought of everything. "I'm coming, Tru. Hold on," she said aloud and turned it on.

Not knowing what channels to have it on, she tried each one. "Mayday?" She wasn't sure if that was the correct call sign but said it anyway. "I need help. Can someone help me? Please?"

Nothing.

Danika changed the channel and repeated her plea. Over and over, she hoped someone would hear her. Her SOS message went out on every airwave, but no response was returned. She closed her eyes and with her lips to the speaker and the button pushed, she did something she'd never done.

"God, I don't know if You will hear this or what frequency You work on, and I know I've never thought I needed You, that I've always attempted to solve my own problems, no matter how long they took, but this is one problem I can't solve, and time is against me. I could sit here and make a deal with You. I could say I promise to go to church for the rest of my life, if You would just zap me out of here, but I suppose we both know that isn't a promise I would keep. I'm just being honest. I've never seen any reason to include You in my life. I suppose I saw how Melinda's faith didn't save her. And I guess, her faith won't save me either. And yet, I find myself still asking, God, if You can hear me, can You help me?"

Danika put the radio down onto the ground, taking her finger off the button. She looked out at the stars over the desert, and even though she had no idea which direction to go, a strange sense of peace came over her. "You *did* hear me," she said in a whisper of awe.

The largest star in the sky twinkled.

Danika couldn't explain how she knew, but whatever happened to her now, she knew she was seen and heard.

Perhaps, that was what Melinda knew as well and why she never feared anything.

Danika picked up the radio to put back into her bag, making the decision to start walking before the sun came up. Just as she zipped the bag back up, the sound of static emanated from it.

"This is Carlsbad Sheriff's Department. Do you read?"

Danika fumbled over the zipper in her rush to retrieve the radio in time. Once again in her hand, she slipped on the button and had to push it three times before she finally was able to speak. "Help me! This is Danika Lewis, and I need help."

"Miss Lewis? I have a tracker on your radio and help is on the way."

She pushed the side button on the radio. "It's not just for me! Tru Butler is trapped in the Lechuguilla Cave. He's at the bottom of Boulder Falls. He needs to be rescued. And you can't trust his ranger team. Someone is sabotaging him."

"Roger that. We'll start our own team. Don't you worry, we'll get him out."

"I want to be there," she said on a rush, not even sure where it came from. But once the words were out, she knew she needed to be. She looked up at the sky again. "He's my lead. I have to be there. I have to follow him out."

"Then you will be."

TWELVE

Tru ran his hand along an edge of the rock that pinned him. Its sharp, jagged edge confirmed his suspicions that this rock had been cut.

He recalled the moment before he felt his rope slip. There had been a grinding sound. At the time, he had thought it was the cave shifting, but now he knew without a doubt that someone had been up there.

And if his gun had been thrown back to him, then that someone must have Danika.

"I failed her," he said aloud and dropped his forehead to the rock in front of him and let its coolness soothe the nausea rolling in him. "God be with her. Keep her safe. Do what I couldn't do."

The exhaustion of guilt overtook him. His attempts to free himself had sapped every drop of energy in him. He felt sleep creeping in and desired nothing but to close his eyes and enter the oblivion. Sleep would be better than the delirious thoughts his choices were bringing on.

But then, he deserved the punishment for leading Danika right into danger.

In his many quests through dark underground tunnels, and tight claustrophobic spaces, he'd seen many people turn to delirium. The mind had a way of shutting down when it couldn't process the bleak reality of where it was any longer; when mind over matter didn't work anymore, and the matter took over.

So this was what that hopelessness felt like.

Tru knew all about misery, grief and anger from the loss of Melinda and his older brother's accident ten years ago, but he had never experienced the feeling of hopelessness over the consequences of his actions. With Melinda he had felt guilty about allowing her to take the lead, but with Danika, he had delivered her right into danger. The feeling of knowing he could never go back and fix what he had done only made him want to crawl under this rock and never come out.

At this point his leg had gone numb. He figured circulation was being cut off to it and wondered if that would cause permanent damage. Not that it mattered, if he was never getting out of there.

He dropped his head back against the wall and closed his eyes. He tried to envision Danika making an escape from her captor. She had the strength. He'd seen it. He imagined her fighting against the faceless man. He imagined her running back to him, and together they would take down that crime ring.

Tru huffed at the absurdity. More like insanity as he slipped into delirium.

"Tru! I'm coming for you. I'm almost there!"

He groaned and let his head fall to his shoulder. Images of her filled his mind and strangely brought him peace. How could this woman just come into his life and take over his mind?

He didn't care. He liked her there. Somehow, Danika Lewis broke through his hard shell, and he was better for having known her.

A new kind of darkness that went beyond the dark cave seeped into his state of consciousness like a growing ink spill. His time of fighting it came to an end.

Something cold jolted him, and he twisted his face away from the assault.

"Drink this," Danika said.

Danika? How? Her voice sounded as if she was in this hole with him again. She could touch his face. He forced his eyes open, but a bright light made him close them instantly. The dark didn't hurt as much.

A loud sound pierced his ears, and he felt vibrations against him. He opened his eyes again and put his hands up to shield the glare away.

"You need water. It's been over twelve hours." The voice came from the direction of the light. As he let his eyes adjust, he took the water Danika offered. It felt so good on his parched lips.

As if it was real.

He lifted his hands and touched the canteen but bypassed it, for her hands were also on it.

Flesh-and-blood hands.

"You're real," he said with a raspy voice.

"Drink now," she ordered with no room to debate.

Tru took his fill, letting the water replenish every dried-up cell in his body. Had it really been over twelve hours? And why was she down here again?

He wanted to ask but the words just wouldn't form on his lips. And that grinding sound hurt his head.

Suddenly, he felt the pressure of the rock fall away. He fell forward with it.

"Whoa," Danika said. "Hold on to me. You're free. They broke the rock up."

That's what the grinding sound was that he just heard. His mind processed this as he tried to move his leg.

She knelt in front of him where the rock had just been. Where he had leaned into the stone, he now leaned into her. No matter how much he tried to hold himself up, he couldn't. It was like every muscle in his body had gone to sleep. Or died.

A sudden realization that maybe he was dead struck him with panic. "Am I...dead?"

"Not yet, you're not. And you won't be." She put the canteen down and placed her hands on his cheeks. Her face was so close, and the glow of her headlamp above them revealed the features of her strong beauty.

He vaguely remembered her asking him if he was going to kiss her. He couldn't place when that occurred, but the idea of dying before he had an opportunity compelled him to push himself forward and touch his lips to hers.

The instant she froze told him something wasn't right. But in the next second, she pulled away and someone else was there, quickly harnessing him on a recovery pulley. He felt the motion of being pulled up out of the Boulder Falls. Before he made it to the top, sleep beckoned, and he drifted into unconsciousness with the touch of her lips still tingling his own.

* * *

The next day Danika sat beside Tru's hospital bed. The doctors had sedated him to allow him to recuperate in his sleep. As far as they could tell, all his tests came back free of any long-term effects. The circulation in his leg would come back. The machines beeped his heart in a steady rhythm while fluids seeped into him through the IV. She herself had dozed off numerous times, and now leaned forward over her forearms on the end of his bed to rest her eyes.

"I didn't expect to see you here," Tru whispered.

She lifted her head and studied his complexion. "I could say the same about you."

"I just mean I thought…"

"That I was never coming back," she finished his sentence.

He shook his head. "That's not what I was going to say. When my gun came back down Boulder Falls…" He swallowed hard; his throat convulsed. "I thought you might be…dead."

"I was taken by someone." She nodded, then shrugged. "For some reason, I'm better alive than dead to these people. The guy dumped me off in the middle of the desert in front of a cave…the cave I apparently am looking for. It's not in Slaughter Canyon."

Tru sat up but quickly fell back to his pillow. He squeezed his eyes and pinched the bridge of his nose. "Too fast." He looked back at her and brought his hand down to the bed. "Was it the right cave? Did you find the evidence of smuggling?"

Danika pushed back to the vinyl chair. "I didn't go

in. Once I was rescued, I wanted to be part of your rescue team."

He tilted his head. "So I didn't dream that you were there? You really did come back down to get me?" At her nod, he said, "Why?"

"Because I don't ever leave my lead."

He scoffed and looked to the ceiling. "Come on, Danika, you and I both know you're the real lead. I may be the guide, but you've been in charge the whole time. I nearly got you killed. I'll find you a new guide as soon as I get out of here. In fact, I'm sure Bard would take you through. If you do find evidence of the smuggling route, he's going to need to know anyway. What do you need me for?"

Danika pressed her lips tight. She asked for this. In holding back the truth of what she was really looking for, she put them both in danger. "I haven't been honest with you. I'm not looking for a smuggling route. I'm looking for a stolen artifact."

He squinted and cleared his throat. Glancing at the table beside his bed he reached for the cup. She jumped up to pour him some water and passed it over to him. Once he lowered it, he said, "Are you looking for this artifact for the person who hired you? Are you planning to steal it yourself?"

"It doesn't belong to me, but I would like to return it to its rightful owners. I would tell Bard about it, but I worry if the government confiscates it, it will never be given back."

"And you think I won't? I *am* part of the government, you know."

"I wasn't a hundred percent sure, which is why I

didn't tell you the whole truth. But now…" Danika captured his gaze. "Now I know I can't do this without you, and I have to take a chance and trust you."

Tru sighed and took another sip. He drained the cup, throwing his head back, and placed the cup on the table. "I want to know who hired you. I need to know that I won't be breaking the law."

She shook her head. "You'll actually be helping me bring justice for a heinous crime. Righting a wrong and returning an ancient artifact to its rightful people."

"Who are these people?"

"The Pueblo People of Taos, New Mexico."

Tru's eyes widened. "The Pueblo Nation hired you?"

"No. Actually no one hired me. I'm working this case for my own personal reasons."

"Why does this sound like a vendetta?" His piercing gaze dared her to deny it.

"I know it looks that way, but it's not for revenge. It's for truth." Danika stood up and went to the end of the bed. She grabbed hold of the base and leaned over it. "I have to do this for my father."

Tru sat still. After a few moments of debating his next words, he sat up slowly, coming closer to her. "Your father, who died. Go on," he said softly.

"The police said it was a suicide, but I know it wasn't. I know he was murdered. And I know he was murdered for the artifacts he found on his last dig. There's a rare headdress in particular that I think got him killed. The authorities said he gambled everything away. That's a lie. He wasn't a gambler. A risk-taker, yes, but not a gambler. His life's work as an archaeologist was taken from him. And then, so was his life."

Her cell phone rang, disrupting them. She pulled the phone from her back jeans pocket and saw it was Brina. On a sigh, she hit the green button. "Brina, I'm not able to talk right now, can I call—"

"No, you will talk right now. You work for *me*, and you were supposed to meet me at the cavern yesterday. I expect you there first thing in the morning. We have things to discuss. Meet me at the main cavern. Do you understand?"

"Of course. I can do that," Danika said, hoping Tru couldn't hear the woman's demanding voice. "I will see you at 8 a.m. We'll talk then. It's going to be great. Bye." She clicked off. "Now, where was I?"

"Stop." Tru held up his hand. "This woman who *thinks* she's getting married in the main cave, who is she to you? What's her part in all this? Why are you bending over backward to accommodate her, even taking her verbal assaults? That is not you. You're too strong for that."

Danika calmed at his words. "That's nice of you to say."

"Nice has nothing to do with it. It's the truth. Which means this woman must have something you need for you to stick around and take her abuse. Why?"

His point-blank question told her she would have to tell him everything. Would he laugh at her ideas of the killers being the Elliot family? Or at least the patriarch of the family?

"You can tell me, Danika." Tru's voice changed to one of support. His urging expression confirmed it.

She took a deep breath, and let it out slowly with, "Brina's father was a colleague of my father's."

"And?"

"And I'm pretty sure he killed him and stole my father's artifacts."

Shock took over his supportive look instantly. Slowly, he leaned back and appeared to be processing this information. "That's a big accusation. What's your proof?"

"All those pictures I took came from his secret vault in his basement."

"Which he gave you the keys to."

Danika dropped her gaze to the bed.

"I thought you said I wouldn't be involved in anything illegal."

She looked up. "You won't. I promise. You're just going to help me get through this cave and find the place I think the artifacts are being kept. That's it."

"And then let you go after a supposed killer alone."

"If it's not him, it is definitely one of the wedding guests. But yes, I will be going after whomever it may be."

"Ah, I get it now. You hope to capture a killer through the lens of your camera."

"That's the plan, and why I need you to approve this wedding in the cavern."

"More breaking the rules? After taking you into Lechuguilla I would think you would see the danger in that. Rules are made to protect."

"I think my father's killer has been protected long enough. It's time to take him down."

Tru tilted his head. "Unless he takes you down first."

THIRTEEN

Tru checked the time on his phone. It was 7:30 in the morning, and he'd been ready to bust out of this hospital room for hours. He knew from overhearing Danika's conversation with Brina last night that they would be meeting in half an hour. He meant to be there. Even if he had to leave without being discharged.

With all the information Danika had shared with him about her father's death and his missing artifacts, Tru spent the night agonizing over what kind of Pandora's box she was about to open. She had explained to him the location of the cave that she was taken to, but he didn't recall it as any of the caves he had ever been in. It sounded as if it was on the outskirts of park property. Nearby Slaughter Canyon but not in it.

And how did she know she wasn't being led to her death? It could very well be a trick. More than anything, he wanted to tell her to let the authorities handle this, but her point that they had the opportunity and they did nothing made him realize she had no other choice.

He stood up off the edge of his bed and walked to

the door. No nurse sat at the station. Strolling out into the halls, he walked down one and then another. As he turned another corner, he bumped into his doctor.

"I have to leave. Duty calls," Tru said.

The doctor looked into his face, studying his eyes particularly. "I was just on my way to discharge you. All your tests came back great this morning, and you're good to go." He opened the file that he held and pulled out a piece of paper. Passing it over, he said, "I'm sure your girlfriend will be pleased to see you looking so healthy. She was quite worried."

Tru realized he was speaking about Danika and wondered what transpired while he'd been asleep. "She's not my girlfriend. We're really not even friends." Saying the words didn't feel right, but they were the truth. An image of her holding his face in the pit of Boulder Falls flashed in his mind.

His kiss flashed next.

When he'd awoken yesterday and realized everything that he remembered happening in that cave was true, he waited for her to mention that kiss.

Nothing.

And yet she was worried about him? To the point the doctor noticed her anxiety.

"Was there anything specifically she said?" Tru asked. He may be up against the clock in getting out of here, but he considered this information pertinent as he made his decision about helping her. She was a stranger to him and could be using him as well.

"Nothing in particular. But I'm surprised the two of you aren't an item. When I told her you just needed rest, tears of gratitude came to her eyes. And she never left your side while you slept. Many times when I walked by, she was holding your hand. When I came in to check on you, she told me of any changes she noticed in you. She was very happy to see your coloring return and even brushed your cheek when she said it. You may think there's nothing between you, but that's not the image I saw. Girlfriend or just friends, that young woman cares about you. Well, have a good day," the doctor said with a smile, leaving Tru to process this information as well.

A bit dazed, he checked his phone again. He called Bard for a ride, and within ten minutes his friend picked him up out in front of the hospital.

"Anything I should know about?" Bard asked as he headed toward the park.

"I'm not sure what I can share with you," Tru replied. "Did you ever have a case that took a turn in a direction you never saw coming?"

"All the time. People think they're covering something up, but the truth will find you out. That's all part of investigating. Did you run into some crazy twist in your cave?" Bard glanced his way and smirked.

"Something like that. I happened upon some illegal activity that may even include a past murder. This fall wasn't a coincidence."

Bard's smirk slipped from his face. "Do you need me to get involved?"

Tru shook his head. "It was on park property, so I really should be calling park patrol. But I just don't know who to trust right now. I had another incident where someone got into my office and damaged my climbing equipment. My team is compromised. And twice now Danika has been put into jeopardy because of it."

"How so?"

"The first time when my equipment didn't work. She had to climb solo out on one of the cliffs. She got to the top and I heard her scream and disappear. By the time I got there, she'd been tied up in the rope and left on the edge of a cliff. And then the second time, she had to climb up Boulder Falls to get help when I ended up pinned down there. Once again, she was taken and put in harm's way."

Bard sent him a sideways glance as he pulled into the park entrance. "And both times she was released?"

"Yeah."

"And both times you didn't see anyone?" He pulled up to the entrance of headquarters.

"Yeah. Why?"

Bard shook his head. "Buddy, are you sure you can trust this woman?"

"That's what I'm trying to figure out."

"Well, don't think so hard about it. She's playing you. In all my days in investigations, I have never seen a kidnapper release their victim twice."

"So you think she's lying to me? That she set up both of these situations on her own to make herself look like a victim." The idea sickened Tru.

"I think this is one of those cases that you mentioned. Things don't add up because someone is sending you on a wild-goose chase. And that someone is Danika Lewis."

"But she seems so genuine. She was good friends with Melinda. She's suffered much loss at the hands of corrupt people. She needs my help." With each reasoning he put out there, Tru realized what he sounded like. "Have I been conned?"

Bard shrugged but nodded. "Looks that way to me. Don't take it personal. She's a beautiful, strong woman, and she is using those features to get something. Any idea what she's looking for?"

Tru dropped his head to the headrest with an exasperated sigh. "Yeah, she's looking for some old Native American artifacts. Claims she wants to return them to their rightful Pueblo owners."

"She needs you all right. Just be careful about taking her down into the caves. Next time you may not make it out. Once she has what she wants, she won't think twice about leaving you behind. She'll disappear into the sunset, and you'll never see the light of day again."

Tru didn't want to believe this, but how could he not? He felt like a fool, captured by a pretty face and a strong physique.

He opened the door and stepped out. "Thanks, Bard. You've talked some sense into me."

"Anytime. You gonna send her packing?"

Tru shook his head. "Nah, but instead of waiting for that twist in the cave that gives her the upper hand again, I'm going to catch her in the act."

Bard laughed. "I'm only a phone call away. And if she really is stealing Native American artifacts, I look forward to arresting her and confiscating all she finds."

Tru shut the door and watched his friend drive off. He checked his time again and knew Danika and Brina were meeting at the mouth of the Carlsbad Cavern. He retrieved a park truck and headed that way. As he pulled up, he spotted the two of them in the crowd of visitors. The side of the park was always packed with people wanting to get a taste of caving but also stay on a paved path.

Parking in an authorized-vehicles-only spot, Tru exited the vehicle and slammed the door. He approached the two of them from Danika's back. Brina noticed him first and smiled.

"I'm so glad you're here," Brina said, and Danika turned his way. "Danika is telling me there're problems with the wedding. She thinks that it could be too dangerous for all the guests. I've been in that hall. It's huge. She wants me to have it in the amphitheater as planned. Will you tell her that's not necessary?"

"Tru, you're out of the hospital?" Danika's eyes glistened with excitement.

She really is an amazing actress, he thought with disdain.

She lifted her arms and wrapped them around him for a hug.

He stood still and did not lift his.

Slowly, she dropped her arms and stepped back. Concern flooded her face. *Or more like false concern*, he told himself. "Is everything all right? Are you still hurt?" She glanced over his body and down to his leg. "Is your leg all right?"

"So many questions," he responded but had to force himself to ignore them. She really didn't care about his well-being. He had to remember that fact, even if the doctor at the hospital thought otherwise.

But why pretend to care if she thought no one was looking?

The doctor had said Danika never left his side, and when the doctor walked by, she was holding his hand.

The whole thing had to be an act, he reasoned.

Or maybe Bard was wrong about her. As an investigator, he could just have a cynical look on life. Criminals had a way of instilling that in law enforcement. Maybe Danika *was* being genuine.

Tru had no way of knowing. He had to keep to his plan and protect himself just in case. Looking at Brina, he said, "Shall we head inside and see where you want your wedding?"

Brina squealed and clapped. "See, Danika, I told you everything would be fine."

Tru stepped up beside Brina and led her inside the cave, leaving Danika behind. He supposed she should get used to it because that would have to be her place from now on.

It had been years since Danika had stepped foot into Carlsbad Caverns. The last time had been with her father on an expedition trip he had in the area. She now walked solo behind Tru and Brina, giving them time to discuss the apparent wedding. She didn't know what made Tru change his mind, and honestly thought he would tell Brina right then and there that there would be no wedding in the cavern. Perhaps their last few harrowing days together gave him a change of heart. She hoped it meant he had decided to help her find her father's killer.

As they left the natural light of the sun and real air,

she stepped foot into an intricate world that curved down pathways of glossy formations and vaulted ceilings that dripped with icicles of stone. She knew the park lost thousands of formations every year due to the many visitors, but the teams of volunteers and rangers had done a fine job of keeping the thousands of visitors each day on the path. She observed a group of volunteers, armed with sponges, brushes and pails as they washed away the footprints of people who left the paved pathways.

Danika expected to feel the pinch of claustrophobia set in. The idea of holding a wedding in a cave had seemed ludicrous, especially after the suffocating confines of Lechuguilla. But Carlsbad Cavern was nothing like that cave. This light, airy cavern invited her right in as it spiraled downward with one splendid view after another. Room names like the Balloon Ballroom and, of course, the King's Palace didn't do these opulent areas justice.

Carlsbad Cavern was magnificent.

Conversations drifted around the rooms as uniformed rangers provided tours to individuals and groups. It looked like a whole school was here on an outing. A baby cried off in the distance.

"Are you even listening?" Brina yelled over her shoulder.

Danika looked away from a formation so stupendous, and forced herself to concentrate on the spoiled woman in front of her. Did she even grasp the wonder of the place?

"Why *do* you want to have your wedding in here?" Danika couldn't help asking.

Brina stopped and huffed Danika's way. "I don't know why that is the business of the photographer, but if you must know I happen to love caving. And so does Terrence."

Brina and Tru continued on. Several more twists, turns and tunnels led the way to faintly lit pathways and noisy areas. There was no baffling silence like in Lechuguilla. And with the crowds came safety too.

"I think I like this cave better, Tru. How about you?" She smiled during her question that she called to his back.

He didn't respond but kept walking.

It was the second time since he arrived that she was left feeling as if she'd said something wrong. When she gave him a hug outside, she felt him not respond. She brushed it off, thinking perhaps he was still in pain. But ignoring her was a whole other matter.

Had he changed his mind about helping her?

She didn't want to jump to conclusions. After all, he was here telling Brina the wedding was on in the cave. He led the way into the Big Room of Carlsbad Cavern. Being the largest room, it would definitely fit everyone.

"I want the King's Palace," Brina said. "It was always my favorite."

"It's the farthest to walk," Tru informed. "But I understand. It is highly decorated with amazing formations. The many draperies and columns make for a stunning backdrop."

Danika followed behind to what was about a mile into the cave. He stepped through four chambers until they reached the deepest portion of the cavern.

"We are 830 feet beneath the desert surface," he said as Brina stepped in and swirled around the room.

"It's even more beautiful than I remembered. Danika, take this picture over here. I want to show Terrence where we'll stand."

Danika removed her camera from her backpack. As she began shooting images, she said nonchalantly, "Where is Terrence? I thought he'd be joining us."

"My fiancé is a very busy man. Besides, I want it to be a special surprise for him." Brina moved around the room, contemplating where people could stand and where she would have the best views.

Tru stood off to the side in silence.

Danika took a few more pictures and made her way over to him. Behind them was a large drapery that felt almost like a veil encompassing them. She waited for him to say something, but he did not.

She leaned her head close. "I want to thank you for going along with this. I know it won't be much longer until I know the truth."

He huffed but said nothing.

"Is something wrong? You've been very quiet since you arrived. Or at least with me, you have been. Have you changed your mind about helping me? Is that why?"

"I'm here, aren't I?" His snide comment raised more flags. Something definitely was wrong.

"Yes, you are. And I'm grateful for that. Thank you." She glanced down at his leg. "I really do care about you. I do hope you are better."

Tru turned his face slightly toward her. It was the

first time he'd looked at her since he'd arrived. "Yesterday, I would've believed that." He faced forward again.

His words stunned her. She moved to face him directly, meaning to demand what he meant by that. She expected to see some sort of arrogant expression on his face.

Instead, all she saw was sadness.

"I don't understand. I thought we..." She could relate to his sadness. "Why do I feel like I just lost a friend?"

"Impossible," he said. But just when he relieved her of that fear, he continued, "We were never friends to begin with."

She felt her mouth hang wide. "I see. If that's how you want it, then that's what you'll get."

"It is. I'm nothing more than a guide." He looked over to Brina, who was approaching them again. "The room will fit about forty people comfortably. How many are on your guest list?"

"I have thirty of the most influential people in Terrence's and my life coming to our wedding. Plus, a few of my father's colleagues as well as Terrence's father's. It will be cozy. But if their colleagues need to watch from the amphitheater, they can."

"I'm going to need to see the guest list. Being that this is federal property, and we don't typically allow weddings in the caves, I will need to have the identification of each person."

Brina pouted. "That is highly irregular."

Tru shrugged. "The amphitheater is still open for all the guests."

"No, no!" Brina replied quickly. "Of course, I'll

get you that. I'll email it to Danika today. Will that be okay?"

When Tru didn't respond right away, Danika thought he might say no. At his nod she relaxed.

A tour shuffled into the room, a large group of people of all ages. Danika and Brina squished closer to Tru as the room filled to its max. As the tour ranger gave the visitors the rundown of the chamber, Brina asked Danika, "Do you have your cell phone on you? I'll email it right now."

Danika removed her phone from her back pocket. "I do, but we don't have service in here." She held up the phone to show it to Brina.

The tour guide spoke from somewhere, but Danika couldn't see him over the many heads of people. He instructed everyone to make sure their phones were turned off because he was about to turn off the lights and wanted no lights to be visible. Danika put hers back into her back pocket, and in the next second, the chamber went pitch black. Not one glimmer of light shone through. The inky darkness seeped past Danika's eyes and into her very being. The absence of light had a way of closing off all her pores and even her lungs. She expected ten seconds of darkness, but time grew. Children whined and adults spoke out in their growing fear.

She understood how they felt.

Danika found herself leaning into Tru, almost as if his nearness allowed her to breathe again. She took slow, deep breaths, inhaling his woodsy scent of aftershave and letting it calm her racing heart. She never knew complete darkness could debilitate her.

Finally, the tour guide turned the soft lights back on and everyone shouted their relief.

Danika remained close to Tru and glanced up and caught him watching her. The sadness she had seen before had returned to his eyes. She wished she could make it go away. "Tell me what's going on," she whispered. "What's wrong?"

His face morphed into a hardness that resembled the rocks around him. "It's time to go," he said gruffly. He swiftly moved past her and led the way back through the caverns without saying another word.

Once they hit the exit and the warm sunshine, Brina said, "Okay, I sent the visitor list. Did you get it, Danika?"

Danika hadn't felt the phone's vibration, and one reach for it behind her came up empty-handed.

"It's gone," she exclaimed and looked to Brina. "Did you take my phone?"

Brina looked affronted. "Why would I have your phone?"

"I was showing it to you last," Danika said but quickly turned to Tru. "Everything I need is on that phone."

Including the images she had taken in Dr. Elliot's basement She had backups on her computer, but she was more worried someone would find the pictures and know she had been the one to break into the vault.

One of these two people had been closest to her in the dark and had the opportunity to swipe it. Right about now, she didn't trust either of them, but after the way Tru had been treating her since he arrived, she trusted him the least.

FOURTEEN

Tru went through the motions of searching for Danika's phone, but he had to question if this was some sort of plight on her part to gain his sympathy again. He kept his guard up so he wouldn't be used again. The fact that she pretended he had taken it irked him more than anything.

Danika Lewis had a lot of nerve.

"We've been through the cave twice," Brina whined. "We're not going to find it. And now you've made me miss my lunch date with my fiancé. He is a busy man and has a lot of work to do before our honeymoon." The fancy woman looked at him. "I sent her the list directly. I did not take her phone. There is nothing else I can do for either of you. May I go now?" She crossed her arms in front of her in a state of annoyance.

Tru would've liked nothing better, but he had a few questions for her. "What does Terrence do for a living?"

The woman lit up, beaming with excitement. "He's in the oil business. He owns a lot of land and drills all over. He recently purchased property here in Carlsbad. That's where he is today. Surveying his new property."

"What's his company called? The park abuts some energy fields." Tru thought of the land beyond the fence in the southern portions of parkland.

"Lindsay Solutions. It's a growing company, so you probably haven't heard of them yet. But you will. Terrence wanted to make it on his own. He could have easily gone into the finance business with his father, but he thinks the real money is in oil and gas."

"Sounds like an innovative man." Tru glanced over to where Danika sat on a bench. The way she gnawed on her lower lip and tapped her foot against the pavement made him wonder if he was wrong about her. She genuinely looked panic-stricken.

As if death was at her door.

Or a killer.

"She looks sick," Brina said. "I mean, it's just a phone. She could go to the store and get another one this afternoon."

Tru knew that Brina couldn't understand the severity of the situation. He honestly couldn't either. It was only yesterday that he learned what was motivating Danika and how she had been willing to break the law for it. If her father really had been murdered, and the killer now had her phone, they would know who she is. Most likely, the next incident wouldn't be a warning.

Tru looked at Brina. "You go on ahead. Thank you for helping us look." He walked past her before she left and headed toward Danika. The moment he sat on the bench beside her, she scooted farther away and partially gave him her back.

"I guess I deserve that," he said solemnly.

"Go away." Her words could have sounded angry, but instead all he heard was sad disappointment.

"I can't do that. For one, you're in danger."

She dropped her chin, seemingly deflated. At least she didn't deny it. "And two?" She angled her head to look his way. Her long hair fell to her lap. "Because we both know your second reason is the real reason."

And he couldn't deny that either.

He glanced around at the massive crowds coming and going from the cave. If he was really concerned about her safety, he wouldn't be letting her stay out here like a sitting duck. "I suppose I have my doubts that you're as innocent in this operation as you have led me to believe."

She shook her head with a look of disgust. "And when did you start doubting me? When I risked my life to come back for you at the bottom of Boulder Falls? Or was it when I had the opportunity to go into the very cave I came here for, but needed to get to you first? That no case mattered until I knew you were safe. Was it then? Or perhaps, it was when I was sitting by your bedside praying for you? Something I have never done for anyone, mind you. So please, Tru, tell me exactly when did I lose your trust?"

"You have to see there have been some strange occurrences of you getting yourself into harm's way and getting out unscathed. Bard pointed out that kidnappers don't just release their victims."

She laughed bitterly. "*Oh*, I get it. *Bard* said. And because of that my word doesn't mean anything to you anymore. Because of that I can't be trusted. Well, you can just go back to your digging in the dirt. I'll find another guide to lead me. Someone who believes me and believes in solving this case."

How did this conversation take such a downward turn? He felt himself spiraling faster than any fall he'd ever taken. Talk about a slipup. "I feel like anything I say is just going to tangle me up more than I already am, but I want you to know I do want to solve this case. I want to get to the bottom of it and put a stop to it."

Danika stood up, looking down at him. "For the record, deciding that I'm the guilty party before you uncover one stone isn't solving the case. That's not how investigation works. It's taken me eight years of digging, and I finally see the light at the end of the tunnel. I won't let you take this from me because your so-called friend has deemed me a criminal without even knowing me. What hurts more, is that you didn't stick up for me."

Danika turned quickly and headed back down the path toward the parking lot.

Tru stood up to go after her but decided it best if he gave her some space. He would follow her to make sure she was safe, and that included down into the cave, but he would do it from afar. As long as she was on his land, she was his responsibility, whether she liked it or not.

"Danika! Wait up!"

Danika heard Brina calling her from off in the distance. She had no plans of slowing down and continued toward her SUV. Part of her wanted to scream, while the other part wanted to cry. She'd never been this close to solving this case, and now she had to find a new guide. And not just to lead her through the treacherous tunnels, but also because of a fear of the dark she didn't know she had. That was the part that made her want to scream.

The part that made her want to cry had to do with the man who had a way of disrupting her life. The first time had been with Melinda.

She couldn't explain how he'd done it again, but he had.

She heard Brina's footsteps on the pavement coming up behind her. "I didn't know the two of you have something going on," she said. "I thought you were just friends."

Danika reached her car and opened the passenger door to throw her camera bag in. She slammed it shut and came around the front. "Tru Butler is nothing to me, friend or otherwise."

"Could've fooled me." She glanced in the direction of where Danika had just come from. "After the way he treated you though, I say forget him. Terrence would never talk to me like that." Brina came over to the driver's door as Danika climbed inside. "But I do hope your fallout won't affect my wedding."

Danika did her best not to roll her eyes. Brina's wedding was the last thing she was thinking about right now. "I can't speak for Tru, but I'm sure it will be fine. If you'll excuse me, I have to find a guide." Danika bit her tongue at her slip. She couldn't let Brina know what she was looking for and that her father was her main suspect.

"Well, look no further. I can take you into a cave. I've been caving my whole life."

Danika pressed her lips to keep from laughing. "No offense, Brina, the cave I need to go into is uncharted. It's nothing like Carlsbad Caverns. There are no lights and no paved pathways. And there's definitely no concession stand or gift shop."

Brina crossed her arms in front of her. "I take offense to your derogatory comments. I happen to be an expert caver. It comes with the territory of being the daughter of an archaeologist."

Danika saw her point, having had a similar upbringing and was always rock climbing. And she saw the images in Dr. Elliot's basement. Caves were a part of his career. It made sense that Brina would have accompanied him on expeditions and digs.

But Brina's knowledge of what her father did also concerned Danika. How much did the woman know about his dealings, legal and otherwise?

"Brina, can you tell me how you would feel if someone found something of one of your deceased relatives and kept it? Or worse, what if they took it out of their grave and sold it?"

Brina's affronted expression said she was offended again. "Like if someone took my grandmother's wedding ring off her in her grave?"

"Exactly. How would you feel? What would you do?"

"I would hunt them down and get it back, of course. Why? Is that what you're doing in this cave? Looking for something stolen from someone?"

Danika was satisfied with the response. But was it

enough to trust the woman to follow her down underground? "Something like that. I need your full confidentiality. You can't tell anyone. Not Terrence, and not your father. I'm looking to advance my photography career. If I find this item, I could make it as a photojournalist. No offense to weddings, but this would be a dream come true."

Brina beamed. "Sounds fabulous! Count me in. Let's do this. And I promise to not say a word. I understand how these things have to be kept under wraps. My father was always so secretive about what he was looking for too. The competition is great."

"Exactly."

Brina glanced back toward the cavern. "What about him?" She nodded her head in the same direction.

Danika looked over and saw Tru standing and watching them. "What about him?"

"Is he coming too?"

Danika shook her head. "He doesn't know the exact location of where the cave is. By the time he figures it out, we'll be far down below."

FIFTEEN

Tru followed Danika's car as he made preparations that would protect her. She may not want his assistance, but he would still make sure she was safe. To do otherwise would make him no better than this killer on the loose. To know the danger that she was about to set foot into and do nothing would make the guilt he felt for Melinda's death seem like an anthill compared to what he'd feel if he stood by as Danika risked her life.

But who to trust?

Someone on his team had to have been compromised, but who?

"Call Stacy," he spoke to his phone as he drove. He wouldn't know who the traitor was until they slipped up. Until then, it would be business as usual.

"What's up, boss? And welcome back. I just heard what happened to you. How many times have you used that rope and never had a problem?" Stacy's cheerful disposition came through the line. To think it was her who sabotaged his climbing gear nearly made him break out laughing. She was his right hand in every survey. If she wanted to hurt him, she had ample opportunity and didn't need to mess with his climbing gear. She could have poisoned his food, and no one would have been the wiser.

"Stacy, I need you to put a site crew together for a survey. Today."

A loud laugh filled his car. "You don't ask for much, do you? What's the hurry? Is someone else stuck in Lechuguilla?"

"No one is stuck. Yet. And it's not Lechuguilla. It's another cave. Uncharted."

"Whoa. Where is it?"

Tru watched Danika take the next right out of the park. "It's not on park property. I don't know the exact location yet. I'm working on it. I just need you to get a team together."

Stacy grew quiet. "Boss? I'm sure I don't have to tell you the ramifications of setting up a site crew on someone else's property. Someone could be upset about you going into their cave uninvited. You know how tempers can flare when territory is seized. Whole wars have broken out because someone took up residence on someone else's land."

"I know. I'm not looking to seize property. Unless, of course, something illegal is going on." Tru kept his eyes on Danika's car and could only hope it would not be her in cuffs at the end of the day. "Can I count on you, Stacy?"

"Always. You don't even have to ask. Give me an hour, and I'll have your team together. I can't guarantee you're going to like who you get on such short notice, but I'll have all the bases covered. Medical support, essential supplies, survey support, etc. Just let me know the location as soon as you have it, and I'll send them all out. And I'll be there too. I wouldn't miss this for the world. Sounds like something's about to go down." She laughed. "Get it?"

Tru smirked and shook his head. He could only hope Stacy was not his traitor. "I get it, Stacy. But listen, keep the reasons under wraps. I don't want to alert anyone just in case this turns out to be nothing." His real reason being that he didn't know who he could trust. He planned to find out quickly by putting everyone to the test.

"Absolutely, boss. Oh, and by the way, call your sister. She's worried about you. She says she tried calling you today, but you're not picking up."

Tru glanced at his phone and saw he did have a couple missed calls. "I was down in Carlsbad with no reception. She must have called then. But honestly, I don't have time to call right now." More like he didn't have time to listen to her lecture him. Luci meant well, but sometimes her quest to find the silver lining in every situation was just wishful thinking. "Would you mind calling her for me? Tell her I'll check in tomorrow."

Stacy grew quiet again. When she spoke, her voice was low with the threat of sadness. "She's the last person that I would tell that to. She knows more than anyone that nobody is promised tomorrow. And you should too."

Stacy ended the call, but her words resounded in the cabin of his car and ricocheted off the walls of his mind. Stacy was right, of course, but he had always been the type of person to retreat, to go into hiding when he suffered a loss.

When his brother, Jett, was in his accident and had lost all memory of his family, Tru had taken a job down here in Carlsbad, far away from Taos and far away from the brother who didn't know him anymore. When Melinda had died in the cavern, he crawled farther and deeper into the earth of that cave, surveying it becoming his entire reason for living.

Or perhaps he was just hiding.

"Call Luci," he instructed the phone again.

"Oh, thank God!" Luci yelled into the phone when she answered. "How could you not call me? Do you have any idea how worried I have been? Tru…" Tears clogged her throat and he couldn't hear the rest of her sentence.

Now he felt like even more of a heel. He wasn't having a good day in the women department. First Danika was disappointed in him, then Stacy was disappointed in him, and now, one of the most important people in his life was crying uncontrollably because of his choice to protect himself by cutting himself off from the land of the living.

"I messed up, Luci," he said. He watched Danika take the next turn down a side street that he was pretty sure led to nowhere.

She's trying to lose me, he realized. He took the same turn, speeding up a bit to catch up with her before she did.

"Yes, you did!" Luci took a few deep breaths and began to calm down. She let out a deep sigh and said, "I'm not ready to lose you. The family is still such a mess, and we need you. It's like there's something missing to make us whole again. We can't move on until something in the past has been fixed. Does that make sense?"

Tru watched Danika take the next turn behind a gas station. "I think I understand. It can be impossible to move on when something in the past must be made right first."

Like revealing a crime and solving a murder, he thought as he watched Danika disappear around the bend in the road. She wasn't into anything illegal. She just wanted to right a wrong. Her father's death was what motivated her and kept her driven to uncover it.

Even if it meant she died trying.

He drove around the bend and didn't see her. He increased his speed to take the next bend but still drove solo on the road. No matter how fast he drove, he couldn't catch up.

Did she lose him?

The idea was unfathomable. There was nothing around but desert and boulders.

"Luci, I need you to pray," he shouted, hearing the panic in his own voice.

"Absolutely! I've been waiting for you to ask me this for so long."

"It's not for me. It's for my..." He swallowed hard. What did he call Danika? She was definitely not an acquaintance anymore. She was more than a client that he took underground. "Friend," he said, but even that didn't sit right. And she would probably disagree with that term right about now.

"What's his name?" Luci asked.

"*Her* name is Danika, and I fear for her life. No, wait." He huffed with a laugh. "I don't fear for her life.

She's the strongest person I've ever met. You should see her, Luce. I think she could actually move mountains if she wanted to. And she *is*. She's actually moving mountains and uncovering some horrible things. I guess what I'm really afraid of is what will happen to her when she does."

Luci became quiet. "Excuse me, I guess I'm a little stunned. But also happy. Whether you want prayer for yourself, or not, I have been praying for you. I've been praying for you to come back to life. To come out of that grave you hide in. This is the first time you've shown any resemblance of life. So, yes, I will pray for your…friend. I will pray for Danika, and I will thank God for her. Because she has done what I couldn't do. She's a gift and an answer to prayer."

She's a gift and an answer to prayer.

"I think she is, Luci. She's both of those things," he said as he drove faster than he had ever driven in his life. "But, Luci, she's also lost, and I don't know how to find her. She's about to go into a very dark place, and I should be beside her. Not in front of her, not behind her. *Beside* her. That's all she wanted, and I didn't see that until…until it was too late. Oh, God, please don't let me be too late."

But with no direction and nothing but the wide-open desert before him, Tru had no hope of finding Danika before she descended into a dark and dangerous world that wanted its secrets to remain hidden.

Danika attached her side pack to her belt and let it hang down against her thigh. Inside, they had everything they needed to descend into the cave. She had an extra rope in addition to the one slung over her shoulder. She had a drill to make necessary holes to be able to attach her anchors. She had a harness and, of course, their helmets and headlamps.

"Do you have tape?" Brina asked as she tied her helmet to her head.

"What do we need tape for?" Danika had never included that in her pack.

A smug expression came over Brina's face. It caused Danika to wonder if she should be crawling through the dark with this woman.

"You're heading into uncharted tunnels with many different offshoots that could lead to nowhere. The best way to make sure you don't get lost or turned around in there is to leave a trail behind you. That way you can work your way back and remove the tape as you do. You can also use a rope if you don't have tape. Although rope will only go so many feet. With tape, you can break off two inches and leave every few feet. Some of these tunnels could be very long. But don't worry if you don't have any. We'll be together the whole time, right?"

"Right," Danika said, suddenly unsure of this whole thing. Never had she thought she would be investigating Dr. Elliot with Dr. Elliot's daughter. What if Brina knew about this cave? What if she had been in it many times before? She could be leading her right to her demise.

But why would she do that? As far as Brina was concerned, she was taking her photographer down into the caves for a photoshoot.

Danika checked her camera to continue to play the

part of a wedding photographer. If she found any signs of smuggling or artifacts, she planned to take many pictures. It wouldn't look like anything suspicious to Brina at all. She put the camera in her side bag in its protective case and was ready to go.

Brina scanned the horizon, squinting toward the road they had come in on. "I do hope no law enforcement saw us come down here. I wouldn't want to be arrested right before my wedding. Thankfully, you lost Tru back there."

Danika followed her line of vision. Brina may be happy that Tru was no longer tailing them, but Danika couldn't negate the fact that it was supposed to be him taking her into the cave, and deep down she still wanted it that way.

"If only he had been more supportive of me." She walked to the mouth of the cave, which really wasn't much more than a mound in the ground. Some shrubbery blocked the opening, but Danika noticed broken branches on them.

Signs that people had come through here, and this was not an uncharted cave as the authorities thought.

She peered down into the darkness and felt her knees grow wobbly.

"You're looking a little green, Danika. I do hope you can hang in there with me. I'd hate to kill you."

Danika glanced up at Brina to see the young woman holding back a smile. "If you think that's funny, it's not."

Brina twisted the nut on the locking carabiner. In what Danika thought was feigned innocence, Brina said, "I have no idea what you're talking about." She nodded toward the opening. "You want to go first? Or shall I?"

Danika's voice disappeared. "You know," she choked out. "Maybe I should wait."

Brina's perfectly sculpted brows furrowed. "Whatever for? We have everything we need for a successful trek. I even brought a knife and a gun in case we come across some snakes or bats." She reached behind her and pulled out a small .22 pistol. "Would you feel better if you held this?"

"Actually, yes." Danika's anxiety cut in half. She checked the cartridge to see it loaded.

"Just don't go pointing that thing at me. You do know how to use it, right?"

Danika looked out at a small cactus about twenty feet away. She took aim and fired the pistol, taking a chink out of the corner of the plant.

"I'll take that as a yes." Brina waved her hand at the hole. "After you. It's only about a five-foot jump. I already measured it. No need to rappel just yet."

Danika placed her booted feet into the hole and hopped down. Brina followed, and once inside she went on ahead a bit to scout the next portion.

"It looks pretty flat for a little while. We'll take it slow just in case it drops off. Keep your light on for now." She led the way in silence, every now and then pointing out any uneven ground that Danika might trip on.

All in all, Brina was a thorough guide.

"Ever consider giving private tours?" Danika asked the back of Brina's helmet.

"Not even once." The woman angled her head to

speak over her shoulder but kept her eyesight on the tunnel ahead. "Do you know what you're looking for?"

"Not a clue, but I'll know it when I see it," Danika replied without giving information away.

"Well, if you think this cave is uncharted, I hate to break it to you. Many people have been through here, and it doesn't look as if it will stop."

Danika tripped but caught herself. How did Brina know this? The woman's words brought on wariness and concern. Danika took notice that no rays of sunlight reached this far in. The only light they had were the beams on their helmets. As if on cue, Brina halted and turned around, blaring her lamp in Danika's eyes.

Danika held up her hand to ward off the glare. "Light!"

"Oops, sorry." She pushed her helmet off to the side, and Danika did the same. Both of them stood in the luminance of each other's headlights. Danika noticed hers was a more yellowish-brown glow than Brina's bright white bulb. She wondered why the difference until Brina pointed behind her.

"We have three choices here." She pointed to her right. "That one goes straight down. The middle one looks like a wormhole, and the third seems walkable, at least for now. Which one would you like?"

"Wormhole?"

"On our bellies. Tight quarters." Brina scrunched her nose up. "I'm game if you are, but…" She made a distasteful expression. "I'd much rather walk upright or rappel."

Danika studied Brina's shadowed face. She seemed more down-to-earth under the ground than she did above. "I have to say I'm impressed with your ability down here. I would never have thought it. I mean… it's just that you seem so…not athletic at all. Well, you get the point. I mean no disrespect. You're just so…"

"Too debutante-like. No worries. It's a family tradition."

Danika shrugged, thinking of the photo that had been on her phone, the row of women dressed in white gowns and holding bouquets in the King's Palace chamber of Carlsbad. "Have the women in your family always been debutantes?"

"Always, as far back as I can remember. It's expected."

A question formed on her lips that had to be asked. But how to do it without raising any flags? "Were any of them cavers, like yourself?"

"My grandmother, actually. I suppose I get it from her, but my mother hated that. She never thought caving was ladylike and worried I wouldn't find a *suitable* husband." Brina flashed a grin in the shadows. "I guess I proved her wrong. Terrence suits me just fine. And he's rich and handsome. What else would a girl ever want?"

Danika ignored the question and said, "I don't think I've met your mother."

Brina shrugged. "Her and Daddy divorced about eight years ago. She moved out of state, back to her family. She's supposed to be at the wedding but we'll see. The only time I ever see her is if I go to New York."

"Wow, she did move far."

Again, Brina shrugged, and her cheerfulness vanished. Obviously, talking about her mother was a sore subject. Danika wondered what had made Mrs. Elliot leave the state, her husband and her daughter behind.

"So, have you made up your mind which trail we're taking?" Brina asked, bringing the topic back to the reason for standing underground in the dark. But Danika filed this information away for later. Mrs. Elliot would have left during the same time as her father was killed. There could be something there to unpack.

"Let's walk," Danika said. "No sense making this more difficult if we don't have to."

Brina laughed. "Afraid of tight spaces, are you?"

"Not at all. I've been in some very tight crevices, and they've never bothered me. It's the dark. I never knew that absolute darkness affected people in such a choking way."

"Mmm…" Brina began walking again, giving Danika her back. "Many people have lost their minds in caves. It's the not knowing your place in the world. It's as if you don't exist any longer."

"That's deep," Danika said and sped up to keep up. "Can you slow down? The farther away you are, I lose sight of you. My light seems to be dimming too."

"Turn it off. Stay close to me, and we'll just use my light. It's better to conserve anyway."

Danika did as she was told. She moved up closer to Brina, but off to the side as much as she could, so she had access to her headlight. A certain odor was also growing stronger.

Were they coming to a bat cave?

Every few feet, Brina stuck a piece of yellow tape

to the right wall. "There's something comforting about those little pieces of tape," Danika said.

Then Brina halted. "Whoa."

"What is it?" Danika leaned over her shoulder to see what was in front of Brina.

"It's a lake or river, or something."

"Seriously?" Danika turned her light back on. It seemed even dimmer than when she had shut it off. But sure enough, about a ten-foot drop led to a pool of black water. Danika angled her headlamp to see farther. Brina did the same, showing it was a long tunnel of this water.

"I guess we have to go back and crawl or rappel, after all." Brina turned around to start back.

"Hold on. I want to get some pictures of this. Maybe my flash will reveal more than our headlamps." Danika removed her camera from her side pack and slung the strap over her head. She didn't want to accidentally drop it in the water below. After a few shots, she checked the window display. "I'm not sure this is water. It looks thick like…"

Danika inhaled.

She had to be wrong in her thinking. Tru would probably laugh at her if he were here for being so ignorant, but…

"Brina, I think this is oil. What do you think?"

No response.

Danika turned toward the path and saw Brina had left her behind. She quickly went down the path to catch up. "I said to wait for me! Brina? Brina!"

Echoes of Danika's petrified voice blasted off the narrow walls and back at her ears. Her lamp barely illuminated two feet in front of her. She put her hand to the wall to find one of the pieces of tape. If she lost her light, she would have to feel her way back.

But after ten feet, she'd yet to find a single yellow marker.

Had Brina removed them?

Danika's headlamp dropped another hue, deeming it nearly useless. Not wanting to shut it off completely, she picked up her steps and ran back the way she had come. She could only hope she was correct. She didn't remember turning off anywhere, but Brina had been leading, and all Danika could see was a foot past Brina's shoulder. The woman could have been walking in circles for all Danika knew.

But finally, she returned to the place with the three choices. Danika let out a deep breath she didn't know she had been holding. She was almost back to the entrance. When she found Brina, she had some things to say to the cruel woman. But this served Danika right for trusting the woman to assist her.

"Danika, get down here!" Brina whispered harshly, jolting Danika. The woman had rappelled? "You've got to see this!"

"No way, Brina. In fact, you can get yourself another wedding photographer. I can't believe you left me back there. And with no tape to find my way back."

"It was straight the whole way, and I had to remove the tape. It could ruin the cave. And don't yell in here. Don't you know loud noises can cause a cave-in? Now, get down here and come see this."

Danika's nerves were shot. After her harrowing race back to this point and the fear of being left behind, she needed to regroup and decide if coming in here with Brina was such a good idea.

And now her invitation to rappel down into a dark void with the woman seemed like a trick.

Danika turned back toward the opening of the cave. Brina could get herself out.

"I'm leaving, Brina. You're on your own."

No response came.

"Brina? Did you hear me?" Danika spoke louder without yelling.

The sound of footsteps came from behind Danika, and she abruptly turned around, clutching her chest at being scared again. "Who's there?" she asked, squinting to see beyond her shadowy lamplight.

A dark figure stepped closer from where it had blended with the walls. Then it spoke, "I'm Ranger Kip Sylvester. I'm part of the site team here to rescue you. But, Danika, you *really* shouldn't have come in here."

The way the man spoke didn't sound like she was about to be rescued. And now he stood in the way of her only exit. Going back to the dead end with the lake wasn't an option. And crawling on her belly wouldn't get her away fast enough. Danika's only choices were to rappel to Brina or attempt to get by this man.

Neither felt right.

She reached behind for the gun at her back. "Let me pass," she demanded.

"I hate to break it to you, but you're never leaving this cave. At least, not alive." His hands reached out for her so fast, but the blast of her gun was faster.

The gun may have only been a .22, but inside the tight confines of the cave, the blast was deafening and painful. Danika screamed as she felt the earth tremble beneath her feet. She lost sight of the man in her lamplight as her legs weakened, and she fell back to the floor.

Dust from the ceiling above fell on her face and in her eyes. Had her attempt to escape only cracked the ceiling above her? Would it come down on her and bury her alive?

Then the ranger grabbed her leg.

Yanking free, she had no choice but to run in the only direction open. She had to rappel to Brina.

Danika crawled over to the rope Brina had anchored and swung out in her rush to escape the ranger.

But was she only jumping from one threat to another?

SIXTEEN

Tru hung up the phone with the sheriff's department. They told him where they'd found Danika when she was taken, so he had a location to give to Stacy and for the site crew. He figured he would make it out there before anyone else as he sped up the truck and drove as fast as he could.

"Do you think you'll need a rescue team as well?" Stacy asked once Tru made the call.

A lump formed in his throat. "It hasn't been that long since Danika would have entered the cave."

"And your point?"

He didn't have one. He knew more than anyone that every second was a risk, and one wrong move could end a life.

"Yes, put a rescue crew together too." He wouldn't say a recovery crew.

Tru mentally prepared for treating this rescue like any other. If he lingered on his feelings for Danika, he would be useless to her.

Growing up on Mount Wheeler and working search and rescue with his brother had prepared him to treat every rescue methodically. Never would he just run into a dangerous situation without a plan and a crew.

And yet, he knew he would do just that when he arrived.

"I'm already too close to her," he spoke aloud, sending up clouds of sand in his wake and thinking of how this woman had infiltrated his life while he wasn't looking. In a cave, he would call that a slipup.

But this felt…perfect. This felt right. He felt like he was alive again. After ten years of hiding, he'd forgotten what living felt like. But that also meant he could feel pain again.

Tru thought about the moment he leaned in to kiss her and she did not return the kiss.

That hurt, even in his delirious and dehydrated state.

Was he still being delirious in his thinking that Danika Lewis was perfect for him? He never knew her as Melinda's friend, but she did know him as her friend's fiancé. That alone would make a relationship with him off-limits.

And why she would never return his feelings.

He let that truth sink in, and it allowed him to take a step back from this rescue. Danika was nothing special to him.

"Yeah, right." Now he knew he was still delirious.

Tru raced ahead to the coordinates the sheriff had given him. As he pulled up, he was shocked to see the cave was on park property, but right on the edge. Out in the distance, he could see the chain-link fence that separated the park from the private property of an oil company.

There was also another park vehicle already there. Tru was glad to see he would have assistance.

Then he saw Kip Sylvester by the cave entrance. The new ranger would be of no help, just like he had held Tru back in the last Lechuguilla survey and made the expedition pointless.

Tru sighed in disappointment. Stacy had said he wouldn't like the team that she put together on the fly, and she was right. He grabbed his side pack from the passenger seat and flung the door wide, jumping out.

"Kip, I'm not going to babysit you on this rescue," he said, approaching the cave. "You don't go in if you can't handle…it." Tru drifted off at the sight of blood on Kip's arm. "Is that a gunshot wound?"

Kip winced and nodded, holding his arm at the elbow. "I'm all right. Just a graze."

"Were you shot at out here?" Tru ushered Kip toward the opening, glancing quickly around for the location of the shooter.

"Back by my car," Kip said. "I ducked and hid, so I didn't see where the shooter went."

"We shouldn't be out here. This guy will come back. Get in the cave, now."

So much for not babysitting the man.

Kip jumped down first as Tru radioed for backup. "We have another active shooter out here. One ranger shot, but stable. I'm going into the cave for cover. Get law enforcement backup. Approach with caution. I repeat, approach with caution."

Tru knew this would delay a site crew from being able to set up now. He should have expected this after the last shoot-out. But it also meant he couldn't wait for a team to go in. He would have to go into an un-charted cave alone.

He jumped down inside. Kip stood off in the shadows of a corner. "Have you seen any sign of Danika?" Tru asked him as he prepped himself with the items in his side pack, placing his helmet on first and turning the headlamp on.

"I—I j-just got here." The man sounded terrified. Stepping close to him, Tru checked for signs of shock setting in. Pupils looked fine, and he didn't see any profuse sweating. Skin was paler, but that was to be expected with the loss of blood. He pulled up his bloody sleeve to see it was just a graze.

"You're going to live but keep pressure on it. It's still seeping." Tru reached down into his pack for the first aid kit, removing a few items Kip would need to administer himself. Tru might need the kit for Danika. "Kip. I'm sorry, but I have to leave you here. Stay hidden in the shadows."

"I want to help. Please."

Tru frowned. "I appreciate your willingness to jump into this rescue, but you would just be holding me back now. I promise, the next one, you are on it." Tru felt dust fall on his face and glanced up.

An unstable cave.

Great.

Things just went from dangerous to worst-case scenario. Time was critical and one hard step could take the ceiling down. It could come down if he *breathed* too loud.

"When backup arrives, tell them the cave is collapsing. No one comes in. Got it?"

"G-got it." Kip wrapped his arm with gauze.

Tru stepped back to leave. "I'm counting on you to keep people safe."

"You won't be disappointed, boss."

Tru walked deeper down into the cave, thinking he might have been too hard on the kid in Lechuguilla. He was glad for this second chance to rectify that. But now he needed to find Danika.

And he couldn't even call out to her.

With every step he took, he was careful to walk softly, but this also couldn't be a Sunday stroll. This place was a ticking time bomb.

It was also man-made.

Tru glanced around the walls and ceilings and saw evidence of carving and digging. This was why he didn't have this cave marked as existing. Someone had been making it, most likely for the smuggling operation Danika was investigating.

She had been right.

More guilt waved over him like a flood. Why was it so hard to believe in people?

Because people always leave.

The answer came in an instant, but it didn't feel right. For the first time, he realized that was a lie. His brother didn't leave him. His family didn't leave him. Melinda didn't leave him.

He left *them.*

In his need for justification, he turned his back on them all as if they never existed in his life. He couldn't even have their pictures displayed, as if they all did *him* wrong.

And he did it again to Danika.

Now the only thing he could do was find her and

help her. Not save her. He had no doubts in her capabilities. If Danika didn't need a guide into the underground, he knew she would solve her case blindfolded.

That's what he should have told her. Not accuse her of lying to him.

Tru came upon a chamber with three outlets. To his left was a walkable tunnel, and when he scanned into the dark with his headlight, a splash of yellow on the wall caught his attention. He stepped closer and touched it.

Tracking tape.

But from who? He had never told Danika about using tape. They never got that far in Lechuguilla to need it. She didn't even have any in her side pack. A few more steps, and he realized there were no more pieces. Only that first piece. Was it placed there to lead someone down the wrong path?

Tru halted, wondering if he should keep going, or go back to the chamber to take another route. She had to have taken one of the three. He didn't see her choosing to slide through a wormhole, not after her claustrophobia revealed itself.

But he did see her rappelling without a second thought.

With no more signs of tape, Tru decided to check the drop-off first. When he reached it, he knelt down and found a rope had been anchored to a boulder. By the looks of its age, it looked like it had been used for a while. He hoped that meant it was secure, because he had no idea how far the drop went…or if the rope would even reach the floor.

Turning around, he took hold and began his descent into the unknown.

* * *

Danika struggled to see a few inches in front of her. Her light barely glowed anymore, and she now had to think Brina gave her this helmet on purpose. When Danika landed and came off the rope, she expected to find Brina. But the woman was nowhere around.

Danika inched around what seemed like a large room with columns and dead-end nooks. Was this what amazed Brina before? It was pretty but nothing like the King's Palace in Carlsbad. Of course, Brina's excitement might have only been a trick to get Danika below.

Danika stayed close to the walls just in case. With her back to them, she moved along slowly and with her senses on high alert.

The shuffling sound of someone coming down the rope froze her behind a wide column. She held her breath to not make any noise, but her heartbeat drummed against her ribs. Her body trembled as it could only be the ranger named Kip coming for her again.

She reached for her gun behind her, even knowing to shoot this off would only finish what her last blast had started. And could bury her alive instantly.

But this man meant to kill her anyway.

With her ear turned, she heard the person come off the rope. They shone their bright light into the room. Danika plastered herself against the column to be kept out of the beacon. But the light gave her the full picture of the room, and before she could stop herself, she inhaled sharply at what she saw in the center of the room.

Her father's crates.

The light beam swung her way at having given her

location away, but before she could run, the loudest blast she had ever heard deafened her ears and had her crouching and screaming. The sound was much louder than her own gun had been, causing the cave to moan and shake as dirt and rocks fell from above. The earth sounded like an angry thunderstorm, but instead of rain, it was pouring down large stones and dirt around her. She needed cover but couldn't focus over the cringing sound.

"Danika!" A voice filtered through the ongoing destruction but sounded so far away and muffled.

She possibly imagined it. Why would Kip be calling her?

The cracking of her father's crates brought tears to her eyes. To have finally found them and have the contents destroyed hurt beyond belief. She heard herself groaning, not caring about being found anymore.

Finally, the rumbling stopped. A few rocks continued to fall and cut into the eerie silence of the aftermath.

A cough came from somewhere in the rubble. No light shone in the room now, and she didn't dare move. Was there even a floor anymore?

Rocks could be heard tumbling as if someone was pushing them aside. Then the light beamed back into the room.

She still clenched the gun in her hand, having never let it go. The dust was so thick on her cheeks and eyelashes, she could barely make out shadows around her. She would be shooting blind if she pulled the trigger. At least she didn't have to worry about a collapse now. Now she needed to be concerned about finding a way out. Was her rope still anchored, or had that wall come down? And what about Brina? Did she survive? How would she pass Kip to find out?

"Stay away from me, or I'll shoot you again," she said with more bravado than she felt.

"Again?" the voice rasped. More rocks tumbled. The light came her way, blinding her.

She held the gun high to pull the trigger.

"Don't shoot. It's me, Tru."

"Tru?" Her voice squeaked in disbelief. She dropped the gun and lifted one leg to climb over a large shadowy rock in front of her. Tears filled her eyes, mixing with the dust on her eyelashes as her arms reached out to the shadows. "I can't believe you're here. Oh, thank God!" She took another step up and over, but she couldn't move fast enough. The light bounced around the room as he moved closer to her too.

Then the cave rumbled again and shook.

"Don't move!" Tru yelled in a harsh whisper. He took his pack off and put it down. "It's not stable. Let me come to you." He took another slow step, but the rock between them groaned, and he stopped.

Danika froze but kept her arms extended toward him. Her fingers opened and closed repeatedly. All she wanted was to hold him, to know he was real and really here with her. That she wasn't imagining him. "What do we do?" Her throat convulsed as she swallowed multiple times to unclog it of tears and dust.

"We solve the problem. This rock is teetering, and we have no idea what's below it. Or not. We could be on a precipice of an endless hole. Too fast, and everything could come crashing down."

"But I need to hold you." Her breathing sounded shallow.

"And you will. I promise." He shifted his headlight to the side, so she could see his outline better. He was standing on a rock. "I'm going to move toward you. You stay right where you are."

She followed his orders even though everything in her said to run to him, to hold on and never let go. She watched him test every place he put his feet, until finally she could see his face. His strong and handsome and determined face.

Determined to reach her and hold her too.

"Hurry," she said, her voice wavering, her hands reaching to him. As soon as her fingertips touched the fabric of his shirt, they curled and fisted the cotton tight. He came closer, and she wrapped her arms around him to pull him to her. Her arms tightened while his enveloped her in such a comforting, secure hold. They may not ever get out of this cave, but in this moment, she felt safe in his arms.

Sobs of relief came out of her mouth as she buried her face into his neck. His pulse there thrummed against her lips and reminded her they were alive and well.

"Shhh, it's okay." He rubbed his arms on her trembling back while the low sound of his voice soothed her and calmed her to silence.

"I'm sorry, Tru. I shouldn't have come in here."

"I shouldn't have ever doubted you. Then I would have been with you, guiding you like I was supposed to. Look at me." He touched her cheek and chin to lift her face to his. The deep shadows couldn't hide the intensity of his gaze. His throat convulsed, then he took a deep breath and said, "I may not have another chance to say this, but I'm so grateful to you."

"Grateful?" It wasn't what she thought he was going to say. Friends were grateful for each other. Family was grateful for each other.

She was hoping for something other than grateful. But how could she think such a thing when he had been in a relationship with her friend?

"Whatever happens, I want you to know you changed my life. You came into it and woke me up. I'm forever indebted to you." He leaned close, and she prepared for a kiss, even if his words weren't a profession of any romantic feelings. But at the last second, he placed a sweet kiss on her cheek.

He moved back, but she wasn't ready to release her hold. "It's because of Melinda, isn't it?" The words fell from her mouth without a thought.

"What is?"

"You can't love me because you loved Melinda, because she was my friend."

He cleared his throat and tilted his head, moving the light beam down and away from her face. He huffed a short laugh. "Honestly, Danika, I barely remember you. I'm sorry if that sounds rude. I was going through some family problems at the time and pretty consumed with my brother's amnesia. Melinda was important to me, but she was also more of a diversion from my problems. Someone who would take the same risks as me as I sought out my grave." He frowned. "Only she found hers." He sighed. "She pacified me because she thought she was helping me. But instead, she was enabling me…not to change. Not to live." His palm cupped her cheek. "But not you, Danika. You showed me what living for something looks like. That life has a purpose, and no matter how impossible a problem looks, it *can* be figured out when you have a good leader. So."

"So," she whispered, still waiting for him to answer her question.

"So, my love for you has nothing to do with Melinda, and everything to do with who you are. You will forever be the strong, beautiful, driven, boulder-climbing and life-changing…" He smiled. "Love of my life."

A deep laugh filled the chamber above them. "Well, isn't this sweet."

"Kip?" Tru turned and spoke.

"Kip!" Danika said at the same time and dropped to find her gun wherever she'd lost it. Her hand patted the rocks and crevices. "Get away! I will shoot you again!"

Kip laughed. "You barely shot me last time at point-blank. I'm not scared that your aim will be true this time. You can't even see me. You'll just end up shooting yourself. Just like your dad. That's what I hear anyway."

"Be quiet! Don't you talk about my dad. He was a better man than you ever will be."

"Danika, what is going on?" Tru asked. "You shot Kip?"

"Yeah, she did. This woman who you professed your love to is using you. She's armed and dangerous. Did you even know she had a gun on her? Who brings a gun into a cave, anyway? She nearly took this place down. Only someone who's here for something illegal would have a gun. Like smuggling artifacts."

A harsh spotlight turned on, causing Danika to lift her arm to shield her eyes. The light shone on her father's crates.

"There's the contraband."

"You're a liar," she said. "I have not smuggled anything." Danika looked to Tru, but his shocked face told her he wasn't so sure. "I guess I'm not surprised," she said in disappointment and looked down to see the gun lying on a rock. But what was the point? She knew she wouldn't shoot it again.

She turned around, and now with the aid of the high-powered spotlight she saw Brina curled up in a doorway to another room. She looked like she was sleeping.

Or dead.

SEVENTEEN

"Brina." Danika stood up on the rock and stepped down onto another one.

Tru reached for her, but as soon as he moved, the cave rumbled. "Danika, don't move," Tru said urgently on a harsh whisper.

"I have to get to Brina."

"Brina's in here too?" What else didn't he know? Tru searched around the room until he saw the woman lying in the tunnel. It didn't look like any rocks had fallen on her, but even something small could have knocked her unconscious.

"She was my guide, but we got separated, or she left me behind. I don't know, but there she is. I don't know if she's alive." Danika pointed in the direction of the dark tunnel. "I have to go to her. What do I do?"

Kip spoke from above, "We need to take this woman in. She's a criminal, boss."

Tru never felt so useless. One wrong move could take down the whole cave on all of them. Brina was hurt, and he couldn't get to her. Kip was demanding justice for being shot by Danika.

Danika had a *gun*?

Tru's world was spinning out of control. For someone so used to being in charge and managing every move people made, this sent his mind spiraling into uncertainty.

But there was one thing he was certain about beyond any shadowy doubt, no matter how minuscule.

Tru studied the upheaval of the room with various-sized boulders that had cracked and dropped from the ceiling. To get to Brina, he would have to climb up and over them the whole way.

No, not him, he thought.

"I can't move, Danika. I'm standing on an unstable boulder that if it shifts, could start another collapse. You're going to have to climb over to Brina, carefully and precisely."

"But what if I step on the wrong rock and do the same?"

"Come on, Danika, I've seen you solve problems before. You know what to do. This is a problem like any other boulder you've ever faced."

He could only hope, or they were all done for.

"Boss? If you're not going to arrest her, I will. She shot me, all because I caught her breaking the law by coming in here." Kip huffed with obvious frustration. At any other time, Tru would have validated the man and slapped cuffs on the perpetrator.

But not this time.

Tru ignored Kip and nodded at Danika. "Go ahead, sweetheart. Do what you do best. I fully support you."

"You do?" Her face showed her shock. It shouldn't

have been there at all. That was his fault, and he wouldn't make the mistake again.

"And I love you," he spoke clearly with no room for any more doubts. "I know that sounds impossible, but I—"

"No. It's perfect." She smiled, at first tentatively, but quickly brilliantly. "Thank you for supporting me. And thank you for loving me."

"Always."

"I can't believe this!" Kip yelled from his place twenty feet above them.

"Lower your voice, Kip," Tru ordered. "Or you'll get us all killed." He looked back at Danika and nodded once. "Go."

It was like a light switch flipped on. One second, Danika was wary in her ability to face this problem, and the next, she became lost in such intense concentration that he thought she forgot that there was anyone else around. She studied each rock before she took one step off the one that she stood on. She glanced to the ceiling and the walls and did mental calculations only she could see.

"What is she doing?" Kip asked.

"Shhh," Tru responded.

"That's it. I've had enough of this." Kip stepped back, taking the light with him.

"Hey!" Tru whispered harshly, his voice echoing through the cavern. "Get back here with the spotlight."

"Sorry, *boss*, you made your choice. Now face the consequences." Kip turned and left the area. Darkness seeped in as Kip moved farther away, and the rocks became shadows in his single headlamp.

"How far can you get in the dark?" he asked Danika, expecting about ten feet only. He shone his headlamp in her direction and found her shadowed outline.

"The whole way," she responded in a monotone fashion, still seeming to be in some sort of mental zone. She leaned down and placed a hand on the boulder in front of her, then lifted up her whole body on it and passed over the stone in front of her, skipping the rock that had rumbled. She put her hand on the next one securely and with success.

Tru blew out a deep breath. "That was amazing, Danika. Keep going."

If she heard him, she didn't let on. Rock to rock, she either climbed, twisted or even jumped as agile as a monkey on a jungle gym.

Then she was gone from his light beam, with only the sounds of her slow and steady breathing to know she was still working hard.

Until even the sounds ceased.

"Danika? Are you all right?"

Moments ticked by as he held his breath for her response. He had no idea if there was a hole that opened up on the other side of those rocks that she could have fallen into.

Then the sound of her voice whispered, "I made it."

His nerves eased. A smile nearly split his face. "I knew you could do it."

Until she said, "I didn't realize learning the truth would hurt so much."

Danika hovered inches over the still body of Brina, trying to see her with the last luminance of her light.

The woman's hands were bunched up by her face as she lay on her side. She looked like she was sleeping. Danika already checked her pulse and found the steady rhythm of her heartbeat.

"She's alive," she said on a whisper. "Unconscious." Her gaze went to the fisted hands by Brina's face. Scrunched up in them were two long feathers. Danika removed them carefully, but already knew what they were.

Ancient eagle feathers.

"Is it safe for me to come over?" Tru called from behind.

"Just skip that rock that was between us. The rest are secure." She hoped it would take him a few minutes because she needed that to calm her anger.

Brina held two feathers from the Pueblo head-dress mask that was in her father's collection. The long feathers, now bent and mangled, were the same black-and-white stripes that made up the head covering portion. Danika looked toward the mound of rocks covering her father's collection and knew Brina had seen it. Touched it. But where was it now? Was it still under the crumbled mess? Had she only been able to grab two feathers before she was hit by a rock and knocked out? If there were any doubts of Brina's involvement in this case, they had just been eradicated.

Brina had known exactly what Danika was looking for.

Tru stepped up behind her and came to his knees. He reached to check her pulse as well. "Brina," he said. His helmet brought more light to their surroundings, and Danika could see blood on Brina's face. He tapped her cheeks a few times until the woman moaned.

"Are those feathers?" Tru asked. She couldn't see his face behind his headlamp, but she recognized confusion in his voice.

"My father's collections are all here. But now they're buried beneath the crumbled ceiling. Except for these two feathers. They were in her hands. She knew the whole time what I was here for. She played me, just as I played her."

"Took…it," Brina said and moaned. She reached for her head. "I can't believe he hurt me."

Danika felt such a stirring of anger that she knew she had to step back. She looked at Tru. "I need a minute to calm down."

At his nod his light bounced then angled toward Brina's face. "Why did you take it? And who hurt you?"

"My…dad."

Danika fisted her hands on her knees. "I knew it! Martin Elliot is a thief and a murderer."

Brina turned her head to the left then to the right, groaning. "No."

"Whether you want to believe it or not, Brina, your father killed my father and stole the artifacts he found. The fact that your father would hit you, his own daughter, should show how callous and malicious he is. I can see why your mother left him. She must've known as well what he did."

Brina tried to sit up, but fell back down, holding her head. Tru moved to help her and got her to be partially upright.

"Can you see clearly?" he asked her.

"No. Everything is blurry. And it hurts."

Tru nodded and spoke in a soothing tone. "I know. Can you tell me your full name?"

"Sabrina Louise Elliot."

Tru sighed. "Everything's going to be okay."

Danika scoffed. "Nothing is going to be okay. Martin Elliot is going to get away with this."

Brina whimpered, then let out a loud, heart-wrenching wail. "My dad didn't do this." She cried louder. "Terrence did! He…hit me." Her voice trembled in between sobs. "He banged my head against a rock. It hurts so much," she cried, but her pain was more than physical.

Danika sat back fully to the ground, the air rushing out of her lungs along with her anger. "Terrence was down here? Did you tell him you were coming?"

She nodded and sniffed. "I sent him a text on the way over. I was just checking in and letting him know where I was going. Then all of a sudden, he was here. A gun went off above, and suddenly a wall fell down, and there behind it were the crates. I had just opened one when he came up behind me. I found the headdress you were looking for, but he took it."

Danika glanced at Tru, who was inspecting Sabina's head wound. "How did you know I was looking for it?" And what else did she know?

"My dad knew you broke into the vault the night of the engagement party. He let you. He said he knew your father and knew what you wanted. But he didn't have it." She flinched when Tru touched her head too hard.

"So he knew all along that his belongings were down here." Danika spoke more to herself as she tried to wrap her mind around this.

"He said your dad put them in a cave, but no one knew where. He's been looking for years. All this time, they were behind a wall."

Danika felt her mouth drop open as if she'd been sucker punched. "Why would my father do that?"

Brina shrugged. "I don't know. Just like I don't know why Terrence hit me." Her voice strained as another wail came from deep within her.

Suddenly, Danika wondered if she was being played by Brina again. How did she know if Brina was telling her the truth about Terrence? Maybe the woman hit herself against the wall or was pretending the whole time.

"How do I know you're really hurt?" The words slipped from her lips like an accusation.

Tru shot her a look as he inspected the woman's head. "She's really injured, Danika. She needs stitches. She's not making this up. And she didn't do this to herself."

Danika looked to the ceiling. "Well, then maybe one of the rocks fell on her. What happened to your helmet?" she asked Brina.

Brina sniffed and looked around, her eyes widening as she took in the scene around her for the first time. "Um… I don't know where my helmet went… I think Terrence took it. What—what *happened* in here?"

Danika nearly scoffed. She bit back the comment she wanted to say. "You mean to say you really don't know?"

Brina sniffed and shook her head. "The last thing I remember is holding the headdress you wanted and before I could say anything, it was grabbed from my hand, and I was thrown back against the wall. He punched me in the stomach, and I think that's when he took my helmet. Then he…" She began to sob again, reaching for her head. "He banged my head against the wall, then hit me with something hard. A rock maybe. His fist. I don't know. Everything goes black after that."

Tru replied, "Judging by the markings on your forehead, I would say he hit you with a gun. And right after that, someone shot off a weapon in here and took the ceiling down. Probably hoping to bury us all alive. We need to get out of here soon. This cave is not stable and could completely collapse at any given moment, with or without warning. And you need medical attention. I left my pack on the other side of the room. I'll bandage you when I get it. Do you think you can climb?"

"I think so." Brina said. The look of worry covered her face as she looked around. "What if Terrence is in here still?"

Tru shook his head and peered at the walls. "Doubtful. He must know another way in and out of here. He didn't come up the rope, because I was over there, and I would've seen him." He helped Brina to her feet, keeping his arm around her shoulders. "Do you think you can walk?"

Danika didn't like this one bit. "How do we know she's telling the truth?"

"We don't," Tru responded sadly. "Just as I didn't know if you were telling the truth."

His comment reminded her that she had just received his honor of trust without having to prove anything to him. How could she not extend that same grace to Brina? She may learn later that Brina shouldn't be trusted, but she would never have regrets for treating someone with kindness and mercy.

Danika stepped up and put her arm around Brina's back. From the other side of Brina, Tru looked over at her and unfastened his helmet. Taking it off, he passed it to her. "Give me yours."

"But there's no light left."

"You need to lead us out of here. I've got Brina. Lead the way, Danika."

She removed her helmet and made the swap. From there, she stepped in front of them and found the easiest route around the large boulders in the room. At the halfway point, she knew she walked over the Pueblo artifacts, now buried and smashed. To learn he put them here himself made no sense. Could she live with never knowing why he made such a decision? *If* he had?

She put her foot down and felt the cave tremble. She froze, realizing she was in the same place as before. Lifting her foot off carefully from the boulder, she said, "There must be some sort of fault line or opening beneath this rock."

"I figured as much," Tru said. "It could be a bottomless pit, for all we know."

Danika tried not to imagine such a scenario. She scanned the wall ahead for direction and inhaled sharply.

"What is it?" Tru asked.

"The rope is gone."

EIGHTEEN

Danika focused on how she could lead them past this point. With no rope and Brina and Tru not being climbers, as well as the danger of climbing on the unstable boulder, she crouched low to consider another way up the wall. Instead, she saw another exit. A very low and tight exit.

"Brina, how are you with going on your belly?"

"I can manage," she said. "Why?"

"I think I see how Terrence slipped out of here. And if he can, so can we." She hoped she sounded convincing, because in truth, the idea of climbing through this mere vertical crack in the wall choked her lungs in fear.

"Are you sure that's safe? What if he's waiting for us on the other side?" Genuine fear threaded through Brina's voice. Maybe she was telling the truth, after all.

Or had a reason to be leading them up the wall. Another ambush?

Danika pushed the negative thoughts from her mind. For now, she would give Brina the benefit of the doubt.

Tru spoke. "You do what you think is best, Danika. I trust you completely."

She smiled his way even though he couldn't see her face behind her headlamp. She was beginning to see why Melinda fell in love with this man. This was the real Tru. The way he cared for Brina so tenderly and now his full support in her made her wonder what it would be like to share her life with such a man. "You must have made Melinda so happy." She spoke her thoughts aloud. But once they were out, she didn't regret them. Honesty felt like the best thing between them at this harrowing point.

Tru sighed for a moment before he nodded and smiled. "I hope so."

With that said, Danika took a deep breath and made her decision. "I don't think we should climb this rock." She nodded and pointed to Tru's left. "The wormhole it is."

She led the way, and once they were all in front of it, they knelt down. "I'll go first. It seems wide enough at this point that if we have to turn around, we can."

At his nod, she climbed in and immediately felt the claustrophobia grip her. Taking a deep breath only pushed up her back against the ceiling of the crevice, making the debilitating feeling worse. After a few shorter breaths, she began to glide through, gripping any jagged stone beneath her to pull herself forward. She heard the others climb in and stay on her heels.

"I'm on the end," Tru said. "But I am still your second."

She relaxed in an instant. She could do this, she told herself and crawled farther in. In her light, she caught something up above, stuck to the ceiling of the crevice. As she neared it, she knew she had an apology to make. She reached her hand up and removed an eagle feather. She found it symbolic that eagle feathers had been used for headdresses for centuries as a show of honor and respect.

"I'm sorry, Brina, for not believing you. I just found a feather, which means Terrence has been through here."

Brina whimpered. "I don't want to see him. What if he hurts me again?"

"He won't." Danika made the promise and meant to keep it. She didn't know why the man was in here, but it couldn't have been for any legit reason. "Has he always been interested in Native American artifacts?"

"No. The only thing he cares about is his oil business."

Danika paused in mid-crawl. "Oil business?" Suddenly remembering that he had some kind of dealings with oil land nearby.

Or so he said.

Tru called, "Is everything all right, Danika? Why did we stop?"

She thought of the images on her camera of the tunnel with the black water in it. She had thought it was too thick for water, had thought it was oil. Is that why he was in here?

"Tru, would anyone ever store oil in a cave?" she asked.

"Um…sure. Our own government does it. They keep the reserves in caves in Texas and along the Gulf. They keep enough to supply the country for thirty-one days in the case of an emergency situation. Why?"

"Because I'm pretty sure there's a tunnel in here filled with oil."

He laughed, then grew quiet. "Really? Are you sure it wasn't water?"

"The smell is pretty bad the closer you get to it. And it's thicker and darker than water. I took some pictures."

"When we get out of here, I'll take a look."

She started pulling again, appreciating his positivity about making it out of here. "At least we know Terrence came this way, which means we're not going to have to turn around."

"And that tells me he knows this cave," Tru said. "Crude oil sure would be something to protect. Even to kill over. Perhaps Terrence and Kip got themselves involved with someone stealing it. Or stealing it themselves. Oil thieves are engaged in a practice known as bunkering. They tap pipelines and siphon off the oil into the wrong direction, typically into their own holding containers, ships, trucks…and even caves. A thief can make ninety grand on the black market in a matter of minutes, depending on how many pinhole taps they install into someone else's pipelines. If they keep the pressure slow enough, they can go undetected for a long time. Years even."

"Who buys stolen oil?" Brina asked.

"Around here, I would say deals are made with the Mexican drug cartels, but it can go international to various militias around the world, groups that need oil to carry out their own illegal activities, like terrorism."

"Terrorism?" Brina sounded like she was going to cry again. "I was going to marry this man."

"I'm sorry, Brina," Danika said. "I can't imagine how you feel right now."

Brina whined, "I can't believe Terrence thought he was going to get away with this. Did he even love me? Had it all been a lie?"

Tru said, "I'd like to know how he knew about this cave."

Brina sighed. "I can answer that. I showed him my father's past excavations. My dad was part of the team that carved this cave and made it passable."

Danika inhaled. "I took a picture on my phone of a photograph of him and a crew. My dad was in that picture. That must have been the same excavation. He was an archaeologist on the team, making sure any artifacts found were secured and returned to their rightful owners."

"Yes, I know. I'm sorry, Danika, but I took your phone. I wanted to see what you were up to. My dad told me you broke into his vault, that you disabled the cameras, but I needed proof."

"How did you know my passcode to even open it?"

"I asked you if I could send you the email of the guest list. You took out your phone to show me you had no service. I watched you put your code in, and as soon as the lights went out, I lifted it from your back pocket. Easy-peasy."

Danika huffed. "You stole my phone."

"You broke into my dad's vault."

Danika supposed she had that coming. "Okay, but we're still not even. You left me behind back there."

"I figured you could rappel without me. But I am sorry. If I had waited maybe Terrence wouldn't have hurt me. Why would he do that for an old headdress?"

"It's worth a million dollars at least. It was my

dad's most prized find, well over a thousand years old. If not nearing two. He was in the process of dating it when...when he was killed."

They all grew quiet as they progressed through the crevice. Danika eased the tension by changing the subject back to the oil. "For Terrence to get away with such a crime, he must have had help."

Tru said, "He had Kip looking the other way on his patrols. And we know he had guards willing to kill. I assume the dead guy was a deal gone bad. Typically, criminal gangs look for ways to earn money other than narcotics trafficking. It could have been someone short on cash. Trafficking oil is playing with the big boys. If Terrence has a tunnel full of it, he's got to be hooked up with a big buyer waiting for it. Which means he must have a way to transport it out of here soon. This is some case you have, Danika."

"Yeah, well, I'm not sure private investigating is something I'm good at. I still don't know who killed my dad. Do you suppose what Kip said had any truth to it? That my dad shot himself, even accidentally?"

"I honestly don't know, sweetheart."

She smiled at his term of endearment. For someone who was so hard-edged when she met him, he really was a softy at heart. She liked that.

But then so had Melinda.

Danika had no business thinking of Tru as anything more than a friend. She would never dishonor her friend like that, even if she was falling in love with the man. When they made it out of here, she would have to make him understand.

The end drew near, and Danika nearly sped up. But

that wouldn't make her a good lead. Slow and steady would get them all to safety.

"You okay, Brina?" Danika asked.

"I'm feeling weak," Brina responded. "My head is still bleeding."

"It's not much longer now. I see the end."

"And then what?" Brina asked.

"We get you to the hospital and get the authorities out here to investigate the cave."

Tru chimed in, "*I'd* like to investigate this cave. And figure out how it was never put into the database. The rangers who excavated it broke the law. I'd like to know who they were, and make sure they're prosecuted."

Danika replied, "I saw a picture of the team. There were eight people in the photo. Seven men and one woman."

Brina said, "If you're talking about the picture on your phone, that was Terrence's mother. His father was also in the picture. I think the other four were park rangers working on the excavation and surveying the cave. But I think they're all dead now."

"All four of them? Tru, when did you start working in the caves?"

"I came on about four years ago. After I left Taos, I went to grad school in Texas for six years. Got a Masters and PhD. Then started on the survey team here at Carlsbad. I don't know if these are the same people I remember hearing about, but there was a group of four cavers that went missing on an exploration before I arrived. A couple years after that I got the job and moved here. Death comes with the territory, so I never thought anything of it. But it makes sense why this cave is not on my map if the whole team who excavated it had perished. The secret died with them."

"Convenient," Danika said. "Too convenient. So, the only people alive in that photo are Dr. Elliot and Mr. and Mrs. Derral Lindsay. That doesn't sit right with me."

"This just goes from bad to worse," Brina said. "These are all the people I adore."

Danika frowned, but there was nothing more she could say to make this better for the woman. A bouncing light ahead told her someone was there.

"I'm turning my light off," she whispered and did so. Sure enough, light filtered into the crevice. "Someone's out there. We may have to wait until they leave." Danika paused, and once the light disappeared, she began moving again, slowly and with limited sound. Her light remained off, so it was a blind crawl where she felt her way.

Then, in less than one heartbeat, someone grabbed her forearms and yanked her out as she screamed at the top of her lungs.

"Danika!" Tru yelled into the pitch dark. Without her headlamp, he couldn't see what happened to her. And with Brina in front of him, he couldn't rush forward to find out. Had she fallen into a hole? Or had someone grabbed her? "Brina, I need to get by you."

"Too bad," she replied.

"Too bad? What's that supposed to...? Oh, I get it." Tru rumbled a bitter laugh. "I should have listened to Danika, after all. She was right about you. If she is hurt in the slightest bit, you will wish you never met me. Now, out of my way." He pushed her aside and rushed forward.

Thankfully, she moved ahead and opened the pathway for him. All he could do was feel his way, but the dark never bothered him.

Until now.

Until this woman brought him back to the light. Danika gave him a second chance at living, and he would make sure she went on to live as well.

With or without him.

Tru lifted his hand to feel when the ceiling opened up. Standing carefully, he stretched to his full height and realized he was out of the crevice. "Danika," he called. He dared not take a step just in case she had gone over a ledge. He reached for the penlight that hung off the side of his belt. It wouldn't give him much knowledge of his location, but it would keep him safe and light a three-foot perimeter around him.

He stepped out to inspect his surroundings. He appeared to be in a tunnel that was about four feet wide and extended in both directions to his left and right. This tunnel also felt man-made, but it was hard to tell with his limited light source.

Tru paused to decide which direction to go in. He heard Brina stepping up out of the crevice and would like nothing better than to leave her behind. But that would go against all he stood for. His desire had always been to keep people safe, no matter what.

"I'm sure I don't have to tell you that your wedding in the King's Palace won't be happening, but I'll still lead you out of here." *And arrest you myself.*

Brina laughed as she stepped up beside him. "Seeing as I know my way around here, I'll actually be the one leading you." She snatched the light from his hand and took the left down the tunnel. "Follow me, if you dare."

Tru glanced back in the opposite direction. He couldn't make it in the dark. And even if he could, he wouldn't leave Danika behind.

Tru had no choice but to follow this conniving woman.

"You better be leading me to Danika," he said in her wake. "And she better be unhurt."

"I don't think you're in any position to be making demands. Stick to making maps. Which reminds me, I'm sure Terrence could use your help in that area. This place is huge."

"There's not enough money in the world, so don't even bother asking."

"That's not how this works. We don't ask." Brina walked on in silence, leaving that comment for him to grasp.

"Who exactly is 'we'?"

No reply came.

Something didn't add up. "Terrence left you back there. You could have died if the ceiling fell on you. He could have killed you when he hit you and put that gash on your head. Or debilitated you for life. Why are you so obligated to him? What does he have over you?"

Still, no response. However, the way she picked up her steps told him he had hit a nerve. She turned the corner, and up ahead, light filtered into the tunnel. It seemed like natural light, which could only mean they were heading outside. Tru glanced over his shoulder into the darkness and hoped Danika wasn't still in there. Facing the exit, he braced for whatever and whomever he would find.

Stepping out into the blinding light, he shielded his eyes for a moment to adjust. Then he dropped his hand slowly to cover his mouth at the sight before him.

A tanker truck was parked under the awning of a cliff. As he peered closer, he realized it was more than just parked. It was hooked up to a pipe coming from the walls of the cave.

Once again, Danika had been right.

But where was she?

Brina walked on without him as he took in the operation going on right under his nose.

Circling around, he saw how the large cavern could probably fit three tankers in here with room to turn around. A tall opening on the other side of the cavern would allow them to drive in and out undetected from above. He wondered how long that tunnel went and where it came out. Obviously not on parkland.

Above him, a large hole allowed for sunlight to stream down and fill the cavern. Its warm natural light gave beautiful brown tones to the walls of the cavern. Under any other circumstances, he would've sat in awe. Instead, he tried to figure out what hole this was. Without his maps and without knowing the vicinity he was in, he wasn't sure. With 119 caves on the park property, and many of them with multiple outlets, this one hole could have gone unmarked.

Or deleted from the system. Especially since the four men that surveyed the cave went missing.

Brina stepped behind the front of the truck and disappeared. Just as Tru took a step in her direction, a rope fell from above.

He glanced up to see someone rappelling down from the top of the opening. He didn't think this was a rescue. At about the halfway point, he realized it was a woman. She was dressed in jeans and boots, a black tank top and a red helmet. Once she landed, and made her way toward him, he believed her to be in her sixties. Her hair had a frosty tone to its blond coloring, and her smile was as warm as the cave. She extended her hand for him to shake.

"Jeanette Lindsay," she said.

Tru just looked at her. "Where's Danika?"

The woman shrugged and dropped her hand. "She's safe. For now. Although, when I learned whose daughter she was, I nearly killed her myself."

"There had better not be one hair on her head harmed."

"That will all depend on you." The woman started walking toward the truck. She stopped and looked back at him. "Follow me."

This was twice now that he had to follow someone else he didn't trust. He'd been down into the deepest and darkest parts of the earth, but he had never walked so blindly.

He reached the front of the truck and came around the other side. "What do you want?"

"I'm sure you can see we have a little enterprise going on. All we need from you is to look the other way and keep this cave off the map."

Tru laughed. "Is that why Dr. Lewis died? He refused to look the other way."

A dark and dangerous flash in the woman's eyes sobered him. "Dr. Lewis made a grave mistake in not partnering with us. But the only person who pulled that trigger was him."

"Because you ruined him? Set him up to look like he was a gambling man who lost everything. If it wasn't for his daughter, who knew her father too well, that would have been his legacy. But no more. I will see to it."

She scoffed. "You won't even get out of here alive to tell one person. I suggest you listen to our deal before turning it down so quickly. When people find your body, they'll just assume you wandered off and slipped in one of your caves." She turned back and walked into the cave where Brina had gone earlier.

Once back inside the darkness, the woman turned on her headlamp and led the way down the corridor. Pipes ran along the side of the wall, and Tru could see this was not an amateur production.

"I guess it's cheaper to steal the oil than it is to buy the land," he said to the woman's back. "Just how long have you been siphoning from the neighbors?"

"It is amazing, isn't it? And to think it all happened by accident. My husband financed Dr. Lewis and Dr. Elliot's archaeological dig eight years ago. When they discovered your neighbors were actually drilling sideways in an attempt to reach the oil on park property, an opportunity presented itself."

"Drilling on an angle over property lines is illegal. And so is drilling on federal park property. A full investigation should have been done."

"That's what Dr. Lewis said." She shrugged and kept walking. "His loss."

"What about the park rangers assigned to the project? Didn't they say something?"

"Yeah, but after we pointed out a few things to them, they came around. For a while anyway. I heard they went missing a few years later while on another project."

"What kinds of things did you point out that would make them go against regulation?"

"You're about to find out how anyone can be bought. Including yourself."

The woman didn't say another word as she led him through narrow tunnels. The unmistakable toxic stench of oil itched his nose, and he did his best not to breathe it in deep. The fumes alone could cause pneumonia and kill. But if Danika was on the other end, he'd risk it.

The sound of heated voices filtered down the corridor. He could hear Brina yelling at Terrence for hitting her.

"I could have been killed! And I still can't believe you left me."

"Sorry, I didn't mean to hit you so hard." Terrence laughed. "Besides, I put you out of the way of where I shot the gun. I couldn't bring you through."

"The ceiling over me could have still come down. In fact, the whole cave could have come down. You could have ruined everything."

"She's right," another man spoke. "Hurting her was not part of our deal."

Mrs. Lindsay walked into the chamber ahead of

Tru, and said, "Dr. Elliot, leading Lewis's daughter to this cave wasn't part of the deal either. But that didn't stop you."

Dr. Elliot straightened up at Mrs. Lindsay's entrance. "I'm sorry. I thought her father might have told her where he put the artifacts. I decided to let her live just in case."

She waved for Tru to step up. "Since she brought us a head ranger, I'll consider your slipup paid in full. But next time it might be more than a gash on your daughter's head. Now, it's time to talk business. Everyone welcome Ranger Tru Butler, our newest member, to the team."

Tru sputtered as he shot a glance around a round open cavern. "You're wrong about that," he said, looking straight at Dr. Elliot. The corrupt archaeologist stood behind his daughter and looked just as distraught as Brina. But if he was the one who kidnapped Danika and led her to the cave, then he was also the one who nearly killed him at Boulder Falls. Tru held no sympathy for the man, or for his daughter. "Where's Danika?"

All eyes turned toward the middle of the room.

Tru followed their gazes. At first, he saw Kip sitting behind some sort of control panel. The traitor turned on a machine, and a loud mechanical sound echoed through the chamber.

Tru took in the railings around a large hole in the middle. Lights had been installed around the room and were dimly lit. For being an illegal setup, it sure was elaborate. As he stepped up to the railing, he glanced inside to see oil being stored in the makeshift vat. Dumbfounded at the sight, he found himself speechless. So much for running a tight ship around here. He turned around, growing angrier by the second.

Then he saw Danika and exploded.

A crane swung out over the vat, and on its end, Danika was harnessed and rigged up over the oil. She looked unconscious from the way her head lolled to the side and her hair shielded her face. Her arms fell to her sides, lifeless. He could only hope she was still alive.

"Take her off there right now!" he yelled, running around to the other side, where Kip ran the crane.

"Kip doesn't answer to you. He answers to me and always has. And now, so will you," Mrs. Lindsay said. "Touch him and your darling will be dropped in right now."

Tru stopped halfway, uncertain of his next move. So this was what being owned felt like.

He looked back at Elliot and Brina and realized Elliot was controlled through his daughter. He did the Lindsays' bidding to protect Brina.

Except, he hadn't killed Danika. He had even tried to scare her to go away the day on the ledge. But she wouldn't be dissuaded.

And neither would he.

"What do you want?" he said, a clipped edge to his voice.

"Your full cooperation, of course," Jeanette said. "From now on, you will do everything I say."

"Never," he responded with a sneer.

She nodded at Kip behind Tru, and the next second the crane plummeted toward the crude oil.

The jolt woke Danika up, and she screamed.

NINETEEN

Danika stared down at a round pool of oil coming her way fast. Instinct had her reaching up to useless air to stop from being dunked. However, the momentum of the drop sent her body closer to the metal arm she hung from, and she used all her strength to propel herself higher, but still it was no use.

"Okay! Okay! I'll do what you say!" Tru yelled out from somewhere in the room.

The crane jerked to a stop, and that was the exact thing Danika needed to give her body the extra power to reach higher.

Still, the crane was out of her grasp. But the rope above her wasn't. One hand made contact. Then the other. She made fast work and pulled her body up higher until her fingers finally touched the cold steel of the crane. She hung from it with both hands.

Now to get up and over it.

"Elliot, kill her," Mrs. Lindsay ordered, leaving no room for negotiation in her lethal tone.

As chaos ensued down below, Danika rushed to swing her body left to right, building the momentum she would need to throw her body up and over. In one swift movement, she was able to get her leg up over the arm of the crane and pull the rest of her body up and over to straddle it. She made fast work of unhooking the harness, so she could shimmy backward and no longer sit over the oil.

But she still had to get down with only the wall, which was not as porous as some of her other boulders. This chamber had been carved out and smoothed.

As Danika made it to the wall, she saw Dr. Elliot had a gun on her. The man followed orders like a robot.

Tru ran up and stood between the gun and her. "I said I would do whatever you want."

"No, Tru!" Danika choked at the sight and his words. What was he agreeing to?

Tru looked her way, a look of pleading in his eyes.

She shook her head for him not to go down this path.

He turned away from her and put his hands up. She thought that was it, that he was surrendering himself for her. But his next words said otherwise.

"Dr. Elliot, you can end this right now. It's obvious that the Lindsays have been blackmailing you for years. You may think that you haven't lost anything by going along with them, but you lost everything anyway. Your wife is gone. Your daughter may still be alive, but they stole her away from you anyway. Look at her. They hurt her anyway."

Dr. Elliot's face made no inclination that he even heard Tru. The man was so owned by his past that he was the near empty shell of his former self. Did he even remember what freedom felt like?

"Dr. Lewis fought with everything he had in him against this corrupted life. He knew bondage was not how we were supposed to live."

Mrs. Lindsay sneered, a maniacal look growing on her face as her anger took over. "Dr. Elliot, you will do as I say. Shoot her down. Now."

Danika ignored her, and, keeping her gaze locked on Tru and Dr. Elliot, she called down, "Don't you find it interesting that these people never do their own dirty work?" As she spoke, she secretly eyed the wall to map out her next moves for solid ground. "Instead, they scout unsuspecting people who are just trying to do something good in their lives, and then take advantage of them. You and my father never set out to live a life of crime. In fact, you set out to right them. You were tired of the thievery of ancient Native American artifacts. You were heartbroken over the fact that many invaluable pieces were never returned to the rightful owners. Don't you remember? You came to excavate this cave not to steal oil, but to make sure anything found here was preserved."

Mrs. Lindsay stormed forward. "And thanks to you, we now know where your father hid the lode. All these years, he hid them behind a wall right here, a wall that came down when you shot Kip. Now, you're going down next!" Mrs. Lindsay stomped over to Dr. Elliot and reached for the gun in his hand.

Dr. Elliot turned the gun and aimed it at Mrs. Lindsay.

She stepped back, but only for a moment. As she watched Dr. Elliot's hands tremble in fear, she began to laugh.

Everyone in the room knew he wouldn't pull the trigger, no matter how much he wanted to. If he had that kind of strength, this would have been over years ago. The truth was, Dr. Elliot was a weak man.

But his daughter wasn't. She only pretended to be.

Perhaps Danika had been going at this the wrong way.

As she moved slowly toward the wall, inch by inch to not bring awareness to her descent, she said, "Brina, you do realize you were used to hurt your father, right? If Terrence loved you, he never would have hit you. Deep down you know that. Look at your father. Really look at him and see how broken he is. Haven't you ever wondered why? This whole scene of blackmail you see here right now is something he's been through, and he gave in to keep you safe. These people do not love you. They've been playing you to hurt your father. They've been using you to keep him in line. The digging that he's been doing for them might as well have been his own grave."

In an abrupt move, Mrs. Lindsay snatched the gun from Dr. Elliot's shaking hand. She quickly turned around and aimed it at him and before anyone could do anything, she fired it.

Dr. Elliot went flying back against the wall and slowly slumped to a sitting position against it.

Brina screamed and covered her open mouth with her hands. "Daddy!" She took a step toward her father but stopped and looked back at Mrs. Lindsay. "Why would you do such a thing?" Her voice screeched, and she looked to Terrence. Her head shook back and forth as the shock of the situation took root and morphed her face into that of a child who just realized they weren't immortal. Her whole existence had been a lie, and now, she had a decision to make.

Mrs. Lindsay still held the gun up, her fingers still on the trigger. In a slow, deliberate movement, she turned the gun onto Brina. "What's it going to be? Your daddy or Terrence. Choose wisely."

Danika glanced over at Tru. The situation had stopped her from descending farther down the wall. *Run*, she mouthed to him. At any second Mrs. Lindsay could turn that gun on him. And she'd already proven she wouldn't hesitate to pull the trigger.

Tru shook his head at Danika. He was refusing to go, to save himself.

She mouthed the word *please*.

Not without you, he mouthed back. He nodded to the wall. She still had at least twenty feet to go. He turned back to the group and said, "Let Brina attend to her father." His words broke into the tension and gave Brina a reprieve from having to answer.

They also gave Danika time to find her footing and descend farther.

Dr. Elliot held his hand over his chest. His head leaned back against the wall as he gasped for air. It was obvious the bullet had punctured his lung, and the man probably didn't have long to live. He lifted his other hand up to his daughter. "I…love…you," he whispered on a rasp of air.

Brina broke down in sobs and ran to her father's side, trying to stop the flow of blood with her hands. She looked to Mrs. Lindsay in sheer panic. "Please," she begged, and Danika only saw how Dr. Elliot's bondage would continue into his daughter's life.

Danika grabbed a crevice on the wall to hang from, but also saw that she was stuck with no place to go from here. The wall was smooth.

She put her right hand out to where she saw a crack, but it was out of her grasp. Looking up the wall, she lifted her right foot to attempt to move it back up, but she needed to go down, not up.

Then her other foot slipped, and she screamed, hanging from her hands only.

Danika's two hands clung to two small crevices, but without chalk, she was already slipping. Her fearful voice carried throughout the chamber, echoing off the walls.

"Hang on!" Tru yelled, his voice growing louder as he ran her way.

As he passed Terrence, the man laughed and mimicked Danika's cries of fear. "Sure, hang on so we can kill you later," he taunted. "Neither one of you is getting out of here."

One of her hands slipped. Danika screamed as she only hung from one now. "Tru! Get out of here. There's nothing you can do now."

"Actually, there is," Mrs. Lindsay said. "It's not too late for him to save you. All he has to do is agree to work for me."

Danika called out, "I would never allow him to make such a choice!" She looked down at him where he stood below her. A deep sadness filled her. "Why didn't you leave?"

He shook his head as he craned his neck to look

straight up at her. His arms were out as if to catch her. She had to be nearly twenty feet high. She could kill him if she fell on him. It was impossible, and they both knew it.

"What's it going to be, Tru?" Mrs. Lindsay asked. "Work for me and she lives."

He didn't budge, but Danika saw his eyes flicker.

She shook her head. "Don't." It was as if she could read his thoughts and see that he was teetering on giving in. After his attempts to convince Brina and Dr. Elliot to not cater to the whims of this evil woman, he was now in their shoes, considering to do the same.

"I have to," he said as his head tilted. "I love you."

"No, Tru, you don't. You loved Melinda, and she would never want you to live a life of servitude." She turned her face away from him and looked toward the wall.

Then, in the next second, she solved her problem.

"Yes, I loved Melinda," Tru spoke as Danika fought a smile of excitement over the map on the wall playing out in her mind. "And I know what it felt like to lose her. She lived life with no fear, but I can't do that if it means losing you. I won't lose you too."

"You're wrong. That's not how she lived. She lived her life knowing that God always had a plan for her. That's why she wasn't afraid. Not even to die. Because she knew if it wasn't her time, God would make a way." Danika looked over to Mrs. Lindsay. "Tru will not be taking you up on your offer. Not now and not ever." She looked back at him with a look of adoration. "I love you too, Truman Butler." Her eyes closed for a brief moment as she took a deep breath.

When she opened them, she nodded and knew what she had to do.

She let go of the wall.

"No!" Tru yelled from below at the same moment the gun went off behind him, fracturing the rock where Danika had just been hanging from.

Suddenly, the cavern began to tremble as Danika fell through the air, plummeting downward. Her arms flailed as another gunshot hit the rock. Then she reached out her right hand for the crevice her eye had caught from above, and just as she was about to fall past it, she caught it, jerking to a complete stop. Now, there was only five feet between her and Tru. He could easily catch her now.

The cave trembled and groaned. The oil began to roll with waves, hitting the side of the vat in sloshes. Rocks cracked and fell from the walls and ceiling.

The cave was coming down.

"Now, Danika! I got you!"

She looked back at him and smiled. Then she let herself go through the air and into his waiting arms.

Tru caught her with ease and held her tight. She immediately wrapped her arms around his neck and held him close. He buried his face into her hair, and she wanted nothing more than to kiss him right there, but time was critical.

Mrs. Lindsay's screams said she knew that as well. "This is all your fault!" She still held the gun pointed at Tru and Danika. She had no idea how they would get past her.

"This cave is coming down," Tru said. "We have to get out of here, or we're all dead."

"It won't," Mrs. Lindsay said. "Not after all the work I've done here." She spoke with conviction, and denial, but the crumbling walls said otherwise. Her maniacal glaze in her eyes told him they were *all* in danger.

"Let us pass. You can stay with your cave if that's what you want. But let us go."

"You are mine. I will own you forever!" she said and leveled the gun at him and pulled the trigger.

Tru stepped in front of Danika as she flinched for the pain of the bullet.

Instead, she heard a scream and a splash.

When she looked up, she saw Brina standing at the railing. Mrs. Lindsay now struggled in the oil, floundering and splashing about trying to save herself.

Tru put Danika down. "Run. There's a rope outside. We'll have to climb." But as they passed Dr. Elliot, they stopped.

He looked at Danika, his face void of all color and remorse in his eyes. Brina came back and sat beside her father. She picked up his hand, completely limp now. "I'm...sor...ry." He struggled to wave his hand away from his daughter. "Take...her. My...daugh...ter. My...love."

"Oh, Daddy," Brina cried and dropped her head on his shoulder.

The cave shook and rumbled.

"We have to get out of here," Tru said, reaching for Brina. "Go with Danika. I'll bring your dad."

Dr. Elliot tried to shake his head but barely moved it. "It's...over. Should...have...been...me. Your...fa...

father…good man." Dr. Elliot let out a deep breath that ceased his life forever.

Brina wailed, but Danika pulled her up. Terrence stood over the vat helping his mother from the oil and Kip stood up from the control panel chair, looking unsure of what to do.

"You stay in here, you will die," Tru shouted over the falling rocks. He raised his hand and dodged a few falling near him.

"If I go with you, I'm done too," Kip said.

Tru shook his head. "There'll be a punishment, but God loves to give second chances." He waved his hand for Kip to get out of the cave, and when he moved, Danika caught sight of the eagle feather headdress by Kip's chair.

Mrs. Lindsay saw it too.

She left her son's side and rushed for it. Even covered in toxic crude oil, the woman wouldn't give up her hopeless fight. Mrs. Lindsay may not even survive the toxicity her body and lungs had just absorbed. Could be days. Or could be long, painful years. "Get your mother outside," Tru yelled to Terrence.

A large boulder fell in the doorway. Any longer and they would all be blocked from ever leaving.

It was time to go.

Danika ran with Brina and Kip toward the mouth of the cave, but when she looked back, Terrence and Mrs. Lindsay were gone.

TWENTY

Danika finished her assent on the rope and climbed free of the cave. Brina climbed on while Kip waited below for his turn. Danika looked down for Tru and noticed him running around the front of the truck with Dr. Elliot slung over his shoulder.

As Brina neared the top, Danika watched how Tru kept looking behind him. When he finally made it to the rope, he yelled up to her, "I lost them. Be careful. They may know another way out."

Danika looked at Brina for the answer.

The woman nodded solemnly. "Slaughter Canyon. Where you found the body. The man had been snooping, and Jeanette had him killed. She thought he had been hired by one of the oil refineries. He got too close."

Danika shook her head at the idea of living such a paranoid life, all to protect illegal activities to begin with. She scanned the terrain around her and saw nothing but hills and flat top canyons for as far as the eye could see. It reminded her of the terrain of Slaughter Canyon. They were close by that cave opening. "They won't get far."

Brina's eyes were bloodshot from all her crying. The former light she had in her that gave her her bravado no longer shone in her. The truth had extinguished all she believed, and Danika was sure Brina didn't know who she was anymore.

"I'll give you your phone back," Brina said as she reached inside her backpack and pulled it out. "You can call for help. It's been off so you should have battery life left."

Danika took it without saying a word to the woman. She turned it on and hoped for service.

She had one bar.

But that's all she needed to make her call to the sheriff's office. With Brina sitting across from her, Danika made the call just as Kip came up out of the opening.

"If this cave goes down, I don't want to be sitting here," he said and ran north. Danika could see it had been Kip that day in the visitor center, standing so close, checking to see what she was up to. She wondered what the Lindsays had on him.

"Can you tell me your location?" the dispatcher interrupted her thoughts.

Danika looked at Brina for her assistance, but the woman had yet to snap out of her shock. "Brina, where are we?"

"Near the Texas line. But Terrence and his mother will come out the small cave in Slaughter Canyon. Kip is running that way now."

No doubt to help them.

Danika shook her head at the uselessness of it and relayed the information to the dispatcher. She was told two teams would be sent out and the area of the park was already surrounded. Stacy Riordan had already called the threat in. No one would be escaping today.

"Someone also needs to go apprehend Mr. Derral Lindsay," Danika told the dispatcher. "He's involved in this, even if he wasn't here."

Brina shook her head. "They'll never catch him. He can disappear in a second. He's probably already long gone. He'll be beachside on a remote island by sundown."

Danika blew out a long breath at the thought of the man behind the money getting away.

"You were right about your father, by the way," Brina said.

As Danika put her phone down her head went up. "How so?"

"He shot the gun, but not at himself. The bullet ricocheted and came back at him. He didn't kill himself. He was defending himself...and my father."

Brina's eyes filled with tears, and Danika knew how this woman, who may have fallen for the conniving ways of Terrence's family, still loved her dad.

Suddenly, Danika felt the rope tug. She looked down and there was Tru, making his way up to her.

Danika moved back to give him room, and when he finally crested the mouth of the cave, she reached both hands for him as he did the same to her. There were no words, only the need to hold on to each other after coming so close to such a great loss.

After a few moments of relief in each other's arms, the earth beneath them trembled. "We have to go." Tru took Danika's hand, but before he moved forward with her, he glanced at Brina and frowned. "I moved your father out of the chamber. I promise you that I will do everything I can to make sure his body is recovered for a proper burial."

Brina sighed and nodded. "I don't deserve that but thank you." Just then, two sheriff's department SUVs pulled up, and Brina walked over to them and turned herself in.

Danika wished there could be another way. She allowed Tru to guide her to the other cruiser and climbed in beside him. She held on to his hand and wasn't sure if she would ever let go. She pushed close to him and rested her head on his shoulder as the deputy drove the car away from this cave that had taken so many lives.

She felt Tru move his head and kiss her forehead. "I'll do what I can to get your father's artifacts as well," he whispered.

She thought of the headdress and shook her head. "I just want to return the headdress to the Pueblo Nation of Taos."

He nodded and whispered, "You will. If you don't mind, I'd like to go with you. I haven't been back to Taos in eight years. I'd like to try again."

She smiled up at him. "I would like that. But if it's okay with you, I'd like to leave the other artifacts where my father put them. He had his reasons for reburying them behind a cave wall. He always said that not everything needed to be excavated. Maybe he felt guilty for unearthing them in there, and it was his way of putting them back in their place." She looked out her window and couldn't even see the cave opening anymore. The majestic landscape of red rock canyons and rolling hills lifted her gaze to the setting sun that gave hope for a new tomorrow. "Sometimes things are better off left buried, so we can begin again."

Tru touched her cheek and pulled her attention to him. "Danika, I meant what I said back there. I love you, and I would be honored to begin again with you. If you'll have me." He leaned close but stopped a few inches away from her lips. His throat convulsed as he swallowed hard to await her answer. The intensity in his eyes told her he was waiting for her permission.

She thought about Melinda and wondered what her friend would say right now.

Suddenly, a laugh bubbled up in her throat as she knew exactly what Melinda would say.

"Is something funny?" Tru's brow furrowed.

She shook her head. "Not funny. Joyful. I love you too, Tru. More than I thought I should or would allow. I wanted to honor my friend, but the best way to do that is loving you with abandon. Just as she would have. She would want nothing less for you. And I know that now."

His eyes shimmered. "It wasn't until you snuck into my life that I even realized I wasn't living." He looked at her lips and pressed his own tight. "I have to warn you, I will never let you go. Wherever you go is where I want to be. I'll be your second for life." He leaned closer but still made no move to kiss her.

She remembered the last time he'd kissed her at the bottom of Boulder Falls. How she wanted to kiss him back but couldn't. Wouldn't.

Maybe now was her chance.

Danika brought her hand to the back of his head and stared into his beautiful, adoring eyes. Eyes that adored her. She knew she looked a fright, but she never felt so loved and so in love. "Marry me," she said. "And we will both be each other's second."

His eyes widened. "Who will lead us?"

"The One who's been leading us the whole time. Leading us to meet, leading us through the caves and leading us to this very moment that will start the rest of our lives together with Him as our guide. What do you say?"

He closed his eyes and sighed. "I say this is one expedition I'm not missing." He opened his eyes. "And I have the perfect place to say our vows, where I know God would approve."

She laughed. "Where's that?"

"The King's Palace, of course."

"But that's not allowed."

He shrugged and looked back at her lips. "I know some people. Danika?"

"Yes?"

He looked at the deputy driving up front who had been doing a good job minding his own business. "I'd like to kiss you," Tru whispered.

Danika rolled her eyes. "I think Melinda was right. You really are too slow." And with that, she leaned up and kissed him with abandon. And he kissed her right back.

* * * * *

*If you enjoyed this story,
look for these other books by Katy Lee:*

Holiday Suspect Pursuit
Amish Sanctuary

Dear Reader,

I am a huge lover of our country's national parks. In fact, I have recently moved to Utah and am enjoying my time exploring the many parks here. As far as Carlsbad Caverns goes, it can feel desolate so far south in New Mexico, away from the big cities and in the middle of the desert, but its beauty really happens below all that sand. The stalagmites and stalactites formed naturally around every turn, each so unique, are just the beginning of things to explore as one travels down toward the center of the earth. One can forget the world above is still going on.

With Tru and Danika fighting to survive in the natural elements underground, they also must fight to stay alive from someone lurking in the dark shadows. Every foot placement must be chosen correctly, or disaster could strike. But Danika and Tru learn along the way that God is their perfect guide, and He has already planned their steps out beforehand. They only must trust and believe.

Thank you for taking the time to read this book. I do hope you enjoyed getting to know Danika and Tru. I pray you find it uplifting and entertaining. I treasure contact with my readers, and you can write me anytime at Katylee@KatyLeebooks.com. My website with other ways to connect is at KatyLeeBooks.com.

Fondly,
Katy Lee

COMING NEXT MONTH FROM
Love Inspired Suspense

TRACKING A KILLER
Rocky Mountain K-9 Unit • by Elizabeth Goddard
The last thing K-9 officer Harlow Zane expected when she and cadaver dog Nell join an investigation is to draw the killer's obsessive attention. But FBI special agent Wes Grey notices she matches the victim profile, and when another look-alike goes missing, they must work together to catch the criminal...before Harlow's the next to disappear.

HIDING IN PLAIN SIGHT
by Laura Scott
Fleeing to her uncle's home is Shauna McKay's only option after her mother's brutally murdered and the murderer's sights set on her. Local sheriff Liam Harland's convinced hiding Shauna in an Amish community will shield her—until an Amish woman who looks like Shauna is attacked. It's clear nobody in this peaceful community is safe...

FUGITIVE AMBUSH
Range River Bounty Hunters • by Jenna Night
While pursuing a dangerous bail jumper, bounty hunter Hayley Ryan barely escapes an attack by the fugitive. Teaming up with rival Jack Colter results in the discovery of another criminal—one who's been missing for years. Can their uneasy partnership—and lives—survive their search for not one but two notorious escaped felons?

ROCKY MOUNTAIN VENDETTA
by Jane M. Choate
With her husband's killer released from prison and dead set on revenge, former US marshal Brianna Thomas's fake identity's no longer enough to protect her and her little girl. Now snowbound in the Rockies with the only person she can trust, ex-marshal Gideon Stratham, she must survive a storm *and* the convict's vengeance.

TWIN MURDER MIX-UP
Deputies of Anderson County • by Sami A. Abrams
After capturing a murder on camera, photographer Amy Baker becomes the next target—and her identical twin is killed instead. Now on the run with her sister's newborn, Amy turns to Detective Keith Young, her childhood crush. But when they discover Keith is the baby's father, can he regain Amy's trust...before the killer strikes again?

ESCAPE ROUTE
by Tanya Stowe
While flying above the Texas border, helicopter pilot Tara Jean "TJ" Baskins witnesses a ruthless murder. Now a deadly gang wants her out of the way. Border patrol officer Trace Leyton—her old friend and the man who once betrayed her—is determined to catch the ring's leader...until the search leads to Trace's family.

LOOK FOR THESE AND OTHER LOVE INSPIRED BOOKS WHEREVER BOOKS ARE SOLD, INCLUDING MOST BOOKSTORES, SUPERMARKETS, DISCOUNT STORES AND DRUGSTORES.

LISCNM0722

*Fleeing to her uncle's home is Shauna McKay's only
option after her mother's brutally murdered and the
murderer's sights set on her. Local sheriff
Liam Harland's convinced hiding Shauna in an
Amish community will shield her. But it's clear
nobody in this peaceful community is safe...*

Read on for a sneak preview of
Hiding in Plain Sight *by Laura Scott,*
available September 2022 from Love Inspired Suspense!

Someone was shooting at them!

Liam hit the gas and Shauna braced herself for the
worst. Her body began to shake uncontrollably as the
SUV sped up and jerked from side to side as Liam
attempted to escape.

They were shooting at her this time. Not just attempting
to run her off the road.

These people, whoever they were, wanted her *dead*.

Just like her mother.

Why? She couldn't seem to grasp why she'd suddenly
become a target. It just didn't make any sense. Tears
pricked her eyes, but she held them back.

After what seemed like eons but was likely only fifteen
minutes, the vehicle slowed to a normal rate of speed.

"Are you okay?" Liam asked tersely.

She hesitantly lifted her head, scanning the area. "I— Yes. You?"

"Fine. Thankfully the shooter missed us. I wish I knew exactly where the gunfire came from." He sounded frustrated. "This is my fault. I knew you were in danger, but I didn't expect anyone to fire at us in broad daylight."

"At me." Her voice was soft but firm. "Not you, Liam. This is all about me."

He glanced sharply at her. "They could have easily shot me, too, Shauna. Thankfully, they missed, but that was too close. And you still don't know why these people have come after you?" He hesitated, then added, "Or why they killed your mother?"

"No." She shrugged helplessly. "I'm not lying. There is no reason I can come up with that would cause this sort of action. No one hated either of us this much."

"Revenge?" He divided his attention between her and the road. She didn't recognize the highway they were on, but then again, she didn't know much of anything about Green Lake.

Other than she'd brought danger to the quaint tourist town.

Don't miss
Hiding in Plain Sight *by Laura Scott,*
available September 2022 wherever
Love Inspired Suspense books and ebooks are sold.

LoveInspired.com